Dark Passage

Paul McCusker

PUBLISHING
Colorado Springs, Colorado

McCusker, Paul, 1958-
    Dark passage / Paul McCusker.
        p.   cm.—(Adventures in Odyssey ; 9)
    Summary: Two eleven-year-old boys discover The Imagination Station,
which takes them back in time to pre-Civil War Odyssey, where they encounter
slave traders and the Underground Railroad.
    ISBN 1-56179-474-0
    [1. Underground railroad—Fiction. 2. Fugitive slaves—Fiction.
3. Slavery—Fiction. 4. Time travel—Fiction.]
I. Title. II. Series: McCusker, Paul 1958-   Adventures in Odyssey ; 9.
PZ7.M47841635Dar 1996
[Fic]—dc20   96-7655
                                          CIP
                                          AC
Published by Focus on the Family Publishing, Colorado Springs, CO 80995.

Focus on the Family books are available at special quantity discounts when
purchased in bulk by corporations, organizations, churches, or groups. Special
imprints, messages, and excerpts can be produced to meet your needs. For more
information, write: Special Sales, Focus on the Family Publishing,
8605 Explorer Drive, Colorado Springs, CO 80920; or call (719) 531-3400 and
ask for the Special Sales Department.

This is a work of fiction, and any resemblance between the characters in this
book and real persons is coincidental.

Editor: Larry K. Weeden
Front cover design: Jeff Haynie and JoAnn Weistling
Printed in the United States of America

97 98 99 00 01 02 03/10 9 8 7 6 5 4 3

Adventures in Odyssey Novel 9: Dark Passage

Author's Note: Most of the details in this story were taken from firsthand, factual accounts of slaves who worked in the South and escaped with the help of the Underground Railroad. Other details were provided by a variety of historical reference works, writings from the time period, and eyewitness sources. To convey historical accuracy and portray the true horror of the slaves' treatment, many words, phrases, and colloquialisms have been maintained.

CHAPTER ONE

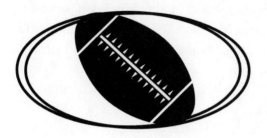

Bang! The door to the hatchway slammed shut. The noise echoed down the dark tunnel and left nothing but a ringing in the ears of Jack Davis and Matt Booker.

"Oh no!" Jack said. The tunnel was so dark that he couldn't see his friend at all.

Matt scrambled up the ladderlike steps, turned the thick, metal handle, and pushed as hard as he could. The door wouldn't lift. "Well, don't just stand there," Matt snapped. "Climb up here and help me."

Jack felt his way up the splintered wooden steps and stopped when he was side by side with Matt at the top. "Quit breathing on me," Jack said.

"You're the one with the bad breath," Matt replied. "Now *push!*"

With grunts and groans, the two boys assaulted the door with every ounce of strength they had. It refused to lift.

"It must've locked when it slammed down," Matt gasped.

"What do we do now?" Jack panted.

If they had been in the afternoon light outside, Jack would've seen Matt scrunch up his nose as he often did when he was thinking. "Scream for help?" Matt finally suggested. He pounded on the door and yelled at the top of his lungs.

"Hold it! Wait! Stop it!" Jack called out to Matt. "Who's going to hear us?"

Matt groaned. Jack was right.

The two 11-year-old boys had been playing catch with a football behind Whit's End, a large soda shop and "discovery emporium" where most of the kids in Odyssey liked to hang out. Jack had gone long for a pass from Matt, but the ball flew over Jack's head and into a patch of woods nearby. While searching for the ball among the fallen leaves and dry branches, Jack stumbled onto a large, metal covering on the ground. It was half covered with leaves. A small sign bolted to the top said to "Keep Out." For the naturally curious Jack and Matt, that meant "Get in if you can." It was an invitation to a new adventure.

Jack had flagged Matt over and turned the latch while both of them yanked at the door. It creaked and opened. A large, black, square hole beckoned them.

"What do you think it is?" Matt had asked.

Jack had shrugged and told Matt to go down and look.

Matt had refused and said *Jack* should be the first to have a peek since he discovered it.

They had argued back and forth for a few minutes until

accusations of "chicken" and "coward" were thrown around. Finally they had agreed to go in at the same time, using a rock to prop the door open for light. But no sooner had they reached the bottom of the stairs and faced the yawning, dark tunnel than the rock slipped and the door closed.

"Maybe we should follow the tunnel to see where it leads," Jack suggested.

Matt snorted, "And get lost in some kind of ancient maze under Odyssey? No way."

"Then let's just follow it a little ways in," Jack said irritably. "If it doesn't go anywhere, we'll come back here."

"And then what?" Matt wondered.

"I don't know. I guess we'll just sit on these stairs until we starve to death."

"That's not funny," Matt said as he crept down the stiff, wooden steps to the tunnel floor.

Jack slowly followed him. "Hello?" he called out, not really believing anyone would call back. He coughed. The air smelled of earth and mildew, like an old basement.

They pressed against the cold, stone wall of the tunnel and inched forward into the blackness. They couldn't even see their hands in front of their faces.

"I heard that a man'll go crazy in a couple of hours in this kind of darkness," Matt said.

"Thanks for the encouragement," Jack growled. "What kind of place is this? An old mine shaft maybe?"

Matt suddenly stopped. Jack walked right into the back of him.

"Hey," Jack complained.

"Watch where you're going," Matt said.

Jack wanted to ask *how* he was supposed to watch where he was going, but he decided against it. "Why'd you stop?" he said.

"If this is a mine shaft, there might be big holes," Matt said in a voice full of worry. "I think we'd better go back to the steps."

Jack sighed. "And do what?" he asked. "Eat wooden-step sandwiches until somebody finds us? I think we oughta—" Jack stopped mid-sentence with a sharp intake of air.

"If it's a snake or a rat, I don't want to know," Matt whispered.

"No," Jack replied. "Look up ahead. It's a little, red light."

Matt squinted deep into the wall of black but didn't see anything. The darkness was simply *dark*. Then the small dot of red light appeared to him as if out of nowhere. "What do you think it is?" he asked. "I mean, you don't think it's anything *alive*, do you?"

"Huh uh," Jack answered. But his tone wasn't confident. "Let's check it out."

Matt didn't budge. "*You* check it out," he insisted.

"Why do *I* have to do everything around here? You're in front, *you* check it out."

"Nope," Matt said. "You saw it first, so you can do the honors."

Jack grumbled his disapproval as he carefully navigated around Matt, keeping his hands on the wall and tapping the ground with the tip of his sneakers to make sure it didn't suddenly open up to a bottomless pit. He listened hard to make sure it *wasn't* some kind of red-eyed monster waiting to devour lost kids. He moved closer and closer until—

Suddenly the red dot turned green.

"Hey," Jack called out to Matt, "the light turned gr—"

Jack heard a soft click, and the tunnel exploded with white light.

CHAPTER TWO

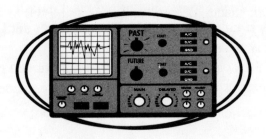

"Ow," Jack said as he winced, covering his eyes with his hands. "Is somebody there?"

"What's going on here?" Matt asked. He squinted against the light and could barely make out Jack's silhouette ahead in the tunnel.

No one answered.

After a minute, their eyes adjusted, and they realized there were floodlights attached to the length of the tunnel wall—from the steps to a door about 20 yards ahead.

"The lights must be motion sensitive," Matt observed.

"Motion *what?*" Jack asked.

"They turn on if something moves," Matt explained. "We have them above our garage. That red light was probably the sensor."

Jack breathed a sigh of relief. "At least we know we're not trapped in some abandoned mine shaft. Let's go see where that door leads."

With renewed confidence, the two boys walked quickly to the end of the tunnel. The door was large and heavy-looking, with square, decorative panels and a round, bronze doorknob. Jack reached out, grabbed the knob, and turned it. The latch clicked freely, and the door opened a crack. "Unlocked," Jack whispered happily.

"You know, there might be somebody on the other side of that door who won't like us barging in," Matt said.

"Do you want to go back to the steps and wait until someone finds your skeleton?" Jack asked.

Matt frowned and said, "The least you can do is knock first."

Jack thought that was a reasonable idea. He ran his fingers through his dark hair nervously, then rapped his knuckles against the hard wood.

"Nobody's going to hear that," Matt said and quickly pounded on the door with his clenched fist. They waited. No one answered.

Jack looked at Matt with a smug expression and grabbed the doorknob again. "Ready to go in?"

Matt lifted his shoulders and raised his eyebrows as if to say, "If you insist."

The door swung open silently on greased hinges. They peeked in uncertainly. Beyond them a workroom, obviously situated in someone's basement from the look of the rectangular windows high on the walls. A dusty sunshine broke through to give the room a warm, orangy glow. Jack and Matt stepped inside.

The muffled sound of kids talking and laughing made its way down the stairs leading up from the room. "We're back at Whit's End," Matt said.

Jack nodded. "This has to be where Mr. Whittaker comes up with all his inventions," he said.

Mr. Whittaker—or Whit, as most people in town knew him—owned Whit's End and ran it as a place where children of all ages could enjoy themselves and even learn something in the process. Whit's End was originally Odyssey's old recreation center, a building that was part house, part church tower, and part gymnasium. Whit completely renovated it to include a soda shop, library, theater, the county's largest train set, and room after room of interactive displays, exhibits, and constantly changing activities.

Standing in the workroom, Jack and Matt suddenly realized just how much time and effort Whit put into his shop. Workbenches littered with tools, electronic parts, and gadgets sat beneath Peg-Boards adorned with schematics, diagrams, cords, wires, safety glasses, and even more tools. Boxes, sawhorses, large drills, a tool chest, and what looked to Matt and Jack like pieces of computer hardware were scattered around the floor. The room was an explosion of half-finished devices, bizarre contraptions, and peculiar equipment—all there for the purpose of helping to make Whit's End a fun and interesting place to visit.

But the thing that caught Matt's and Jack's attention was a large machine sitting in the center of the room.

"What is it?" Matt gasped as he circled the odd-looking

invention. It looked as if someone had combined an old telephone booth with a helicopter cockpit. Through the smoke-colored glass, he could see multicolored lights blinking inside. A low, constant hum seemed to vibrate through his chest.

"Maybe it's one of those booths that takes your picture," Jack suggested. "You know, like they have at the mall."

Matt shook his head. "No way. Why would Whit invent something he could just *buy?* It's some kind of ride."

Jack, who circled the machine from the other direction, nearly tripped over a large cable. It ran from the invention over to a large box that looked like a washing machine. On second glance, Jack realized the "washing machine" was some kind of computer. "Check this out," he called to Matt.

Matt was at Jack's side in an instant. "This is great! The computer must be feeding information into the ride," Matt said. He gazed at several books, encyclopedias, magazines, and newspaper clippings scattered on a nearby workbench. They referred to the Underground Railroad, slavery in America, and the Civil War. Jack picked up one particular headline that reported Odyssey's "November Riots." The year 1858 was handwritten in the upper-right-hand corner.

"This is *great!*" Matt repeated. "It must be some kind of Civil War ride." He dashed around to the door of the machine. "I love that time in history."

"Really? I didn't know that," Jack said offhandedly. History wasn't one of his strong subjects.

The door didn't have a handle, so Matt had to look for a

way in. "My great-great-great-great-great-grandfather was a slave," he said simply.

Jack did a double take as if realizing for the first time that Matt was black. "You're kidding," he said. "You mean he was a slave, like on one of those plantations in the South?"

"Uh huh."

Jack scrubbed his chin thoughtfully. He had never thought much about skin color—his own pale, pink flesh or the honey-brown tone of Matt's. They were friends, and that seemed to be enough. Their parents never drew attention to the difference in their races, either. Why should they? But the thought of Matt having someone in his family who was once a slave made Jack uneasy. What if *his* great-great-great-great-great-grandfather was a slave owner?

"Aha!" Matt exclaimed as he pushed a button. *Whoosh!* Just like an elevator, the door on the "booth" slid back and disappeared into the side of the machine. Jack suddenly realized what was happening.

"What are you doing?" he asked as Matt climbed in.

"I want to see what it does," he replied.

Jack glanced around nervously. "What if Mr. Whittaker comes down?"

"Then we'll get in trouble," Matt said with a shrug. "But we'll still be the first ones to try his new ride."

Jack couldn't argue with his point, so he smiled and squeezed in on the chair next to Matt. It was large and comfortable. They faced a dashboard of buttons, small lights, and digital displays. "This is amazing," Jack said. He picked up a large sheet of blue paper with crude sketches of the machine, numbers, lines, and, on the bottom, the words *The Imagination Station (Revisions & Improvements)*.

"The Imagination Station?" Matt mused. A red button— larger than the rest—beckoned them. "Let's push this one and see what happens."

"Are you sure it's worth it if we get in trouble?" Jack asked.

Matt smiled and said, "We won't know until we try it, will we?"

For an instant, Jack understood why their parents complained that the two boys weren't good for each other. He dismissed the thought and said, "Push it."

Matt poked at the red button with his finger. It clicked down. Nothing happened.

Disappointed, Jack slumped a little in the seat. "Maybe Mr. Whittaker hasn't finished it yet."

Matt was about to answer when the door quickly slid shut with another *whoosh*. The machine made a low, rattling sound that soon got louder and louder.

"It sounds like it's going to fall apart," Jack said, worried.

Matt reached for the red button. "Maybe I should stop it," he said.

It was too late. The Imagination Station shifted into a higher gear with a shrill, whirring sound.

Jack opened his mouth to speak, but his breath was taken away as the machine lurched forward. *Or did it?* Neither of them could be sure. All they knew right then was that it felt as if they had just been blasted out of a rocket silo into warp-speed hyperspace. Butterflies danced in their stomachs. Their eyes were big as dinner plates.

The colors of the lighted dashboard, the smoky glass, and the workroom beyond spun out of control. Jack and Matt cried out.

Then everything went dark.

CHAPTER THREE

This is weird," Jack said in the darkness. He was on his knees, but he didn't know how he got that way.

"*Too* weird," Matt replied from Jack's left. "We're back in the tunnel again."

"Are you sure?" Jack asked, but all his senses told him it was true. The cool earth beneath him, the smell of damp, and the endless night ahead and behind him confirmed it.

Matt patted the tunnel wall with the flat of his hand. "It's the tunnel all right," he said. "But I can't figure out how we got back here."

"Maybe we've been stuck here for hours and only dreamed about Mr. Whittaker's workroom and The Imagination Station and—" Jack stopped himself. Two people couldn't have the same dream, could they? "You remember the workroom and the machine, right?"

"Uh huh," Matt answered. "That's what makes it so weird. How could we be sitting in the machine and the next second be in the tunnel again?"

Jack suddenly gasped and reached out. His hand collided with Matt's chest.

"Ouch! What's wrong?" Matt asked.

Jack shushed him. "Don't you hear those voices?"

Matt listened for a moment. Muted, almost unhearable voices drifted down the tunnel. They were quiet, as if someone had left a radio on somewhere.

"This way," Jack said as he felt his way forward into the tunnel. He looked for the red light that had signaled the motion-sensitive lights. It wasn't there. Instead, he saw a thin, yellow line stretching across the ground and up the tunnel wall. As his eyes adjusted, he realized it was light coming out from under the bottom and side of a door. By the time they were only a few feet away, they could see its outline completely. The door was slightly ajar. The voices were more distinct. Two men were arguing.

"This is *really* weird," Matt whispered as they got closer. Together the boys huddled at the crack in the door and peered through. The workroom was completely different from the one they'd seen before. The workbenches were gone. In their place sat a couple of sleeping cots covered with ragged wool blankets. The walls were bare wood and stone. In the center of the room, a scarred wooden table and wooden chairs crouched on fragile legs. Two men stood on opposite sides of the table. Jack and Matt didn't recognize either of them. One was a tall, slender white man with salt-and-pepper-colored hair that stuck out in wavy tufts. He wore a clerical collar atop a blue shirt and trousers. The other man was taller and stockier. His coat, shirt, and pants were an ill-fitting patchwork that made him look even larger than he was. His face was dark brown and glistened with sweat. He shifted nervously from one foot to the other while clinging with both hands to a frayed hat.

"Is this the basement to Whit's End?" Matt whispered.

Jack shrugged. "I think so . . . I don't know. Listen." They turned their attention to the argument inside.

"No, sir, Reverend Andrew," the black man was saying. "I'm tired of running. We're free now, and I won't hide in someone's cellar. No, sir, I won't."

The clergyman spread his hands in appeal and said with a soft English accent, "Listen to reason, Clarence. They'll catch you and take you back to your old master. That's what they're paid to do, and that's what the Fugitive Slave Law allows them to do. Even here."

The man called Clarence tightened his grip on the hat. "With all due respect, Reverend Andrew, I'm tired of laws that take away a man's freedom."

"So am I," Andrew said sadly. "But what you or I want makes no difference for the moment. Odyssey is in the midst of an all-fired argument about slavery. Douglas and Lincoln have everyone riled up from their debates. The town is split in two. My advice to all the runaway slaves is to keep moving north. None of the American territories is safe. You won't be truly free until you get to Canada. So tomorrow morning, we have to get you back on the Railroad and—"

Clarence interrupted, shaking his head slowly. "We can't take another step," he said. "Not so soon. We've come a long way, and we're tired all to pieces. I have to think of my daughter here."

"It's your daughter I'm thinking about as well," Andrew said as he gestured behind him. Jack and Matt took a couple of steps to the right to get a clearer view of who they were talking about. A black girl—about the same age as Jack and Matt—sat quietly on the edge of a cot. She was wrapped in rags that barely passed for a dress and coat and looked as if she might fall over from lack of sleep. Their movement caught her eye. She squinted at them.

"Somebody's at the door," the girl said softly.

Wanting to hide in the darkness of the tunnel, Jack pushed back against Matt, who stumbled and fell backward to the ground with a grunt. Jack then tripped over Matt and found himself flat on his back in the dirt.

Hands seemed to come from everywhere and hauled Jack and Matt to their feet. Instantly they were both dragged into the room and dropped onto the rickety chairs. Andrew and Clarence leaned into their faces with expressions full of accusation.

"Who are you?" Andrew demanded. "Why were you spying on us?"

"We weren't spying," Matt stammered.

Jack tried to explain, "We got lost in the tunnel and couldn't figure out where we were—er, are. We were just playing football and—"

"We thought we were in a machine in Mr. Whittaker's workroom," Matt chimed in, "but then we were in the tunnel again and—"

"Do you know what he's talking about?" Clarence asked Andrew.

Andrew shook his head no. "Beats the thunder out of me."

Clarence turned to Matt and said, "Where's your papers, young 'un?"

"My papers?" Matt asked.

"Are you free or running away?" Andrew asked.

"I don't understand what you mean," Matt said.

"Come now, son. Where are you from?" Andrew asked.

"Odyssey."

"I've never seen you around Odyssey," Andrew challenged him.

"He *is* from Odyssey!" Jack shouted, mostly for effect. "And so am I! And if you don't let us go right away, our parents are going to send the police here, and you'll be arrested for kidnapping."

"Kidnapping!" Clarence exclaimed.

"Yeah, *kidnapping!*" Matt added.

Andrew waved his hands as if trying to bring calm to the confusion. "Wait just a minute," he said. "Nobody is being kidnapped. Look, lads, I know everyone in Odyssey. So just tell me who your parents are and I'll make sure you get home safely. But first I want you to tell me how you found the entrance to the tunnel. It's important that—"

"Somebody else is here," the little girl said.

All eyes went to the door. Another black man stood in the half-shadows. "I'm sorry to bother you," the man said as he shyly stepped into the room.

"This has turned into a major thoroughfare," Andrew said with a hint of chagrin.

Clarence couldn't mask his alarm. "Just what's going on here?" he asked. "Who are you? Are you all together?"

Jack and Matt vigorously shook their heads. "We've never seen him before," said Jack.

"No, sir, those boys aren't with me," the stranger replied. His outfit was worn and dirty like Clarence's, and the sweat-stained hat on his head drooped down as though it were terribly sad about something. "I'm a runaway slave who's come to you for help because I heard you were part of the Underground Railroad. Have I come to the right place?"

Andrew was about to answer when suddenly Clarence interrupted. "Where are you from?" he demanded. "How did you hear about the Railroad?"

"I'm from Hattiesburg, where any slave with a good pair of ears has heard about the Railroad," the stranger explained. "I've been on the run for weeks."

Clarence eyed him skeptically. "You look awfully healthy for a man who's been running for weeks."

A sliver of a smile crossed the man's face. His eyes narrowed humorlessly under the brim of the hat. "I can't help how I look," he said. "Why're you asking me so many questions? Did I understand wrong? I thought runaways were taken care of here. Aren't I welcome?"

"Of course you're welcome," Andrew said.

"Don't trust him," Clarence said boldly.

"What?" Andrew asked, startled. "Why not?"

Clarence kept his eyes on the stranger as he said, "There's something wrong here."

"Don't know what you're talking about, sir," the stranger said.

"Clarence, please explain yourself," Andrew insisted.

"I've learned never to trust a so-called slave who'd approach a white man without taking his hat off first," Clarence said.

"You doubt this man because of his hat?" Andrew asked incredulously.

"I'm telling you, sir, that it's one of the first things any slave learns. You always take your hat off around white folks. It's a habit. It stays a habit your whole life. The only ones who don't know it aren't really slaves." Clarence stood up to his full height as if he expected the stranger to jump at him.

The stranger chuckled and took his hat off. "Maybe we do things differently in our part of the country," he said.

"Maybe you do," Clarence said. "And maybe you're a free black man who's working for the slave hunters. Maybe you're one of those treacherous snakes who pretends to be a slave to help the slave hunters find the stops on the Railroad. Maybe this is how you find the fugitives!"

"You've no call to speak to me that way," the stranger said. "I think you must be sick with a fever."

"I can settle this," Andrew announced, then gazed at the stranger. "Tell me who sent you here. If you've been traveling on the Railroad, I'll know who told you to come."

The stranger frowned and said, "I don't ask for names, sir. It was an old woman—in a cabin about a mile this side of the Mississippi."

"That would be Mrs. Cunningham," Andrew said with a smile. "Keeps bees to make her own honey, I believe."

"Mrs. Cunningham. That's right. Kept bees. I remember now. Gave me some of the honey," the stranger said, obviously relieved.

Clarence folded his arms and grunted his unspoken doubt.

Andrew seemed satisfied and held out his hand. "Come on in," he said. "Forgive us for being so suspicious."

The stranger took a step forward and shook the Reverend Andrew's hand. "Thank you, Reverend," he said.

Suddenly, Andrew's eyes turned cold as he tightened his grip on the stranger's hand. "Peculiar that your hand doesn't have calluses," he said. "I've never met a slave who didn't have callused hands."

The stranger's eyes widened. "I was a house slave," he explained.

"Really now?" Andrew questioned as he pulled the stranger closer. He continued in a low, threatening voice, "That may be true. But unfortunately for you, there's no Mrs. Cunningham who keeps bees. I made it up."

The stranger jerked his hand away from Andrew and,

with his other hand, put two fingers in his mouth and let out a loud, shrill whistle. Immediately, somewhere deep in the tunnel, men shouted. Oil lamps danced like fireflies in the darkness.

"It's a trap!" Clarence cried out.

"Run!" Andrew shouted. "Run for your lives!"

CHAPTER FOUR

Everything happened at the same time. The stranger leapt at Clarence in a flying tackle, and the two crashed onto the table. It collapsed under their weight with a wrenching, splintering sound. The girl screamed. With surprising power, Clarence grabbed the stranger, rolled him over, and delivered a hard blow to his jaw.

The Reverend Andrew grabbed Jack, Matt, and the girl and pushed them to the stairs. "Run!" he shouted.

"Daddy!" the girl cried out.

Clarence jerked his head around and yelled, "Go, child! You know where to meet me!"

Andrew spun to face the crowd of men as they appeared in the tunnel doorway. The girl and Matt raced up the stairs. Jack followed, but not without first seeing the men from the tunnel pour into the room, their lamps and guns lifted. They descended like a pack of wolves onto Andrew and Clarence.

"What in the world's going on here?" Matt called over

his shoulder.

"I don't know," Jack shouted back, "but I sure hope Whit's End is at the top of these stairs."

Matt and the girl reached the top landing and disappeared around the corner. As he reached the doorway himself, Jack wished he would find himself in the soda shop, with Whit serving ice cream behind the counter and kids crowded into every booth, table, and corner. Whatever he and Matt had done by getting in The Imagination Station and pushing that red button—whether it was a weird dream or some kind of ride—Jack was sorry and wanted to put an end to it now. He didn't like being chased by strange men in a strange place. He didn't like the feeling that he and Matt had gotten themselves into something they wouldn't get out of easily. *Please, please, please,* he thought, *let it be Whit's End.*

Jack stopped dead in his tracks. It *wasn't* Whit's End. To his surprise, it was a modest-sized church with stained-glass windows, wooden pews, and, on the far end, an altar, podium, and choir loft.

Matt stood a few feet away from Jack, and they shared the same open-mouthed expression. "Where are we?" Matt asked.

"Don't you know?" the girl asked, bewildered.

They weren't given time to answer, as another group of men burst through the double-doored entrance to the church. "Get them!" one of the men shouted.

Instinctively, Matt, Jack, and the girl ran in the opposite direction, toward the altar. There they found a door that led to a small room filled with books, chairs, and choir robes. It looked to Jack like a small Sunday school room. Slamming the door behind them, the three fugitives looked around wildly. There weren't any other doors out.

"We're trapped," Jack gasped.

Matt fumbled with the door handle, hoping to find a lock. It didn't have one. "Oh, great," he said.

More shouts and the sound of pounding feet on the hard church floor approached.

"What are we going to do?" Jack asked in a shrill voice.

"We didn't do anything wrong, did we? Let's talk to them!" Matt suggested.

"I don't think they're the listening types," Jack replied.

"This way," the girl suddenly said as she climbed on a chair. A small window peeked out at them from above a tall wardrobe. By the time Jack and Matt reached her, the girl already had the window open and was squirming out like a rabbit from a hole. Matt was next. Jack took up the rear, just getting his head and shoulders through when their pursuers exploded into the room.

"Stop!" one of them shouted. Another man knocked over a chair and scrambled after Jack. His hands reached out and caught the edge of Jack's jeans. Jack kicked out at him. The rubber sole of his sneaker grazed the man's chin. With a curse, the man fell backward into his friends. It gave Jack the time he needed. Like a rocket, he shot out of the window, falling to the ground with a heavy thud. Matt helped him to his feet and half dragged him away from the church.

A meadow stretched out before them to a thick patch of woods about 20 yards away. Near it sat a burned-out shell of a house. All was quiet. Jack was surprised that, in spite of the commotion inside the church, no one seemed to be waiting to catch them outside. The girl was halfway across the meadow and beckoned them to follow.

"Well, Matt—where to?" Jack asked, blinking against the afternoon sun.

"Wherever *she's* going, I guess," was Matt's reply.

The two boys ran after her.

Jack felt like a frightened deer as they ran through the forest, scattering fallen leaves, tripping on branches, and leaping over giant logs. A breeze moved the tops of the trees in steady crashes that reminded Jack of waves on a beach. They slowed down only when they were sure they weren't being followed. Jack collapsed against a log and clutched his aching side as Matt fell into a pile of leaves.

"No," the girl said, "not yet. We have to go on. It's not far."

"What's not far?" Jack groaned. The girl hardly seemed winded. Where did she get the energy?

"Come on," she said and jogged onward.

Matt rolled his eyes and struggled to his feet. "Guess we'd better go," he said as he stumbled after her.

Jack pushed off the tree and dutifully followed.

They crossed a large field that was autumn brown and baking in the sun. It felt soothingly warm after the coolness of the woods. Jack wanted nothing more than to lie down right there and bask in it. But the girl continued on relentlessly. They soon came upon another thicket that was abruptly scarred by a dirt road. Crossing it with careful looks in both directions, they entered a small copse, and, finally, the girl stopped in a clearing within sight of the road.

"Here?" Matt puffed.

"You're kidding," Jack panted, his dark hair matted against his skull.

"My daddy and me said we'd meet here if we got split up. We passed it on the way to the reverend," she said simply.

Jack and Matt looked warily at each other. They were standing in the middle of a small assembly of wooden crosses, small grave markers, and gray tombstones.

"A *graveyard?*" they asked together.

CHAPTER FIVE

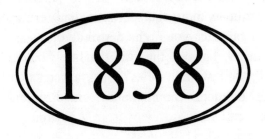

Agraveyard," the girl said with a nod as she sat under a tree. "Daddy said I'd remember it—and I did," she added proudly.

Jack looked around for a church, a house, or anything else that might explain why there was a cemetery in the middle of nowhere. "This is weird," he said. "Why are these people buried way out here?"

"I asked my daddy," the girl answered, "and he said these folks were probably buried out here because they died of some kind of disease."

"Oh, *great*," Matt said as he moved away from the solemn gathering of the dead.

"Forget about that," Jack said as he stooped next to the girl. "I want to know what's going on here. What happened back at the church? Why were those men chasing you?"

"*Us*. They were chasing us, too," Matt amended.

"Yeah."

The girl looked from Matt to Jack and back again. Her expression made them feel as if they'd just stepped off a spaceship from another galaxy. She suddenly frowned. "How do I know I can trust you?" she demanded.

"You mean, besides the fact that we've been running together for the last three miles?" Jack asked sarcastically.

The girl pondered the idea and seemed to agree with it. "My daddy and me ran away from Alabama. Those men wanted to take us back, I guess."

"Why did you have to run away from Alabama?" Matt asked. "Did you escape from jail or something?"

She smiled for the first time, her teeth yellow and crooked. "Heavens no," she said. "We ran away from our master."

"Your master?" Jack asked.

"Yes, sir," the girl replied. "He was really mad because my mama ran off to Canada, and he swore he'd make me and Daddy pay for it. He was going to sell me down the river. So we ran away first chance we got. Been using the Underground Railroad the whole way here. We're going to Canada to meet Mama."

Jack scrubbed a hand over his face. "This doesn't make any sense," he said.

The girl looked earnestly at Matt. "You don't act or talk like any slave boy I ever met before. Are you a runaway, or are you free?"

"I'm free," Matt said as though the girl were crazy.

Jack stood with his hands on his hips, his brow furrowed.

"What happened to us?" he asked Matt. "One minute we're in a tunnel, then we're in Whit's workroom, then we're in The Imagination Station, then we're in the tunnel again, then we're running for our lives. *What happened to us?*" His voice bounced from the trees to the cemetery and sounded unusually loud.

Matt's eyes suddenly grew wide. "I have an idea," he said. He spun on his heels and raced over to the grave markers. He seemed to be looking for something in particular as he went from one to another. He finally stopped and gazed down at a tombstone.

"What are you doing?" Jack asked impatiently.

Matt waved him over. "Here. This one looks new."

Jack joined him. "What?"

Matt pointed to the tombstone. *Safe in the arms of Jesus*, it said in carved letters that curled at the ends. Underneath was the name Josiah Slade, followed by the birthday: June 4, 1824. Under that, it said: *Departed this life the 10th of October, 1858.*

"New?" Jack said. "It's over a hundred years old."

Matt slowly shook his head.

The truth hit Jack so suddenly that he whipped around to the girl. "What's the date?" he called out.

The girl had been sitting with her eyes closed. She opened them wearily. "Date?" she asked.

"You know, like on a calendar? The *date?*"

The girl looked perplexed. "I don't know the date. The leaves fell, we had a full moon the other night . . ."

"What year is this?" Matt asked more gently.

"Oh, that." She frowned for a moment, then said, "It's 1858, my daddy said in the summer. I guess it still is."

Jack paced nervously. "I don't believe it," he told Matt. "You're saying you think that somehow we went back in time to 1858? No way. Not a chance."

"Do you have a better explanation for everything that's happened?" Matt countered. "The Imagination Station, Jack. It's some kind of time machine. We're back in 1858, probably Odyssey."

The girl agreed, "This is Odyssey. I saw the signs when we walked in. I can read, you know."

"No way, no way, no way," Jack said as he paced nervously between the graves.

Matt wandered back to the girl. "That's what happened," he said. "The reverend is part of the Underground Railroad—"

"Everybody keeps talking about a railroad, and I don't know what they're talking about," Jack said.

"You never paid attention in history class," Matt rebuked him. "Don't you remember the stories about Harriet Tubman and Frederick Douglass? The Underground Railroad was the secret way runaway slaves got out of the South. There was a whole network of people and houses where the slaves could stop to get food or a place to sleep. It stretched from the South all the way to Canada." He nodded to the girl. "That's how you got away, right?"

"Uh huh," she replied.

Matt went on, "So the reverend is part of the

Underground Railroad, and those guys that suddenly showed up were like slave hunters who catch slaves and take them back south."

"How can they do that?" Jack said urgently. "I thought once the slaves got to the North, they were safe." He seemed to hope that by proving Matt wrong on that one point, it would prove his whole crazy theory wrong.

Matt opened his mouth to answer, but he closed it again. He was clearly stumped.

"The law," the girl interjected. "I don't know the name of it, but when I was a little girl, they made a law so the slave hunters could go north and take the slaves back to their masters."

"See?" Matt spread his hands. Case closed.

The girl frowned and stood up to look around. "Where's my daddy?" she asked.

"I'm sure he's okay," Matt said. "I'll bet he got away and is running here right now." His voice betrayed him, though. He didn't believe it.

Jack shoved his hands into his jeans pockets and turned away. It was still too much for him to believe. How could Whit create a machine that sent them back in time? But the evidence—and his own senses—told him it must be true.

Matt was at his side before he realized it. "Let's go into Odyssey to see if we can find her father," he suggested. "And maybe we can figure out how to get back to Whit's End."

It sure beats waiting around a graveyard, Jack thought. "Yeah, sure," he answered.

"You can't," the girl said to Matt.

"Why not?"

"You're a Negro," she said, as if that answered the question in full.

"So?"

"Do you have any papers that say you're free?" she asked.

Matt was indignant. "No! Why should I carry around papers to say that?"

"Because the slave hunters will think you're somebody's slave, and if you can't tell them whose slave you are or show them papers that prove you're free, they might take you."

"They'd better not!" Matt snapped. "I don't have to prove anything to anybody!"

"Yes, you do," the girl said softly. And it was in the soft resignation of her voice that Matt knew she was absolutely right.

"Better not take the chance," Jack affirmed. "I'll go into town. Maybe I'll find the reverend, and he can tell me what's going on."

"Okay," Matt said unhappily.

There was a silent moment as an expression passed between them like a shadow. It wasn't as if Jack were running to the store to buy them a couple of sodas. There was unknown danger ahead, and they both knew it.

"It's only Odyssey," Jack offered.

"Yeah. Only Odyssey," Matt said.

Jack strode away, lifting his shoulders and picking up his

pace just to show them he wasn't afraid. When he reached the edge of the trees that led to the road, he paused and turned back to them. He shrugged with embarrassment and called out, "Which way is Odyssey?"

CHAPTER SIX

S omething nagged at Jack during the two-mile walk to Odyssey. Apart from getting lost because he couldn't find anything he recognized to guide him, he kept thinking something was different about the world he was now in. Eventually, the ringing in his ears solved the mystery.

It was the silence.

In a world without cars, trucks, buses, or passing jets, the silence was deep and seemed to go on forever. The forest whispered its life through birds singing, leaves rustling, and branches rubbing dryly against each other. The air carried the soft sound of wind, waving grass in the meadows, the yawning moo of a cow, and the occasional snort of a roaming horse. The crunch and scrape of Jack's sneakers against the dirt road seemed out of place, and it felt as if all living creatures for miles around must be wondering what the awful racket was.

Jack was eventually relieved to hear the teapot whistle of

a distant train. Then he came upon houses scattered distantly on both sides of the road, some no more than large, single-storied cabins with plank-floored porches. Most had wooden sheds and outhouses in the back, bordering modest fields and farmland. One woman, wearing a long dress and apron, her hair up in a bun, smiled and waved at Jack as she pinned flapping sheets to a clothesline.

Soon the number of houses increased, along with their sizes and sophistication of design. Simple, square boxes evolved into more elaborate styles with rounded turrets, arrowlike eaves, circular porches, ornamental windows, and chimneys that jutted up from the rooftops. Brick, stone, and nicely painted siding replaced plain wood. Fences sectioned off each property. *The houses are bigger, but the land is smaller,* Jack thought. Crudely painted signs offered rooms for rent, cheap rates at boarding houses, piano lessons, and an attorney-at-law.

"Welcome to Odyssey," a large, wood sign said. Jack couldn't believe his eyes as he got closer and closer. He followed the road—signposted as Main Street—which broadened out from a ruddy dirt path to a thoroughfare smoothed over with paving stones. The clip-clop of horses' hooves and the rattle of wagons and carriages came and went. Houses yielded to tall, square buildings and businesses. Jack strolled down a wooden walkway, passing the displays for barbers, dentists, blacksmiths, shoe and boot repairs, tin shops, saloons, a general store, and dozens of other shops and offices long-since gone from Jack's Odyssey.

From Jack's point of view, Odyssey—even the *world*—
of 1858 was like visiting another planet. There were no
fast-food restaurants or convenience stores on this street;
the store windows contained no microwaves, appliances,
radios, televisions, videos, computers, or even hand-held
calculators; he saw no telephones or booths to put them in;
no electric lights hung above the doors or on the lampposts.
He suddenly realized that almost all the things he would take
for granted hadn't been invented yet.

A group of boys abruptly rounded a corner and nearly ran
straight into Jack. "Watch it," he said.

"Sorry, mister," a freckle-faced boy said, then stopped to
look at Jack long and hard. Adults might not notice a strange
boy walking in town, but kids noticed when someone their
age was around whom they didn't know. "You're a stranger
here," the boy said.

Jack sized him up, just in case the boy wanted to fight. He
was a couple of years younger than Jack. "I'm just visiting,"
he answered.

The boy eyed Jack up and down. His gaze rested on
Jack's jeans and white sneakers. The other boys also noticed
them and whispered among themselves. Jack thought he
heard them say something about "new Levi's" and "queer
shoes."

"They're the trousers that got rivets in them," one boy
said with a laugh.

The freckle-faced kid looked at Jack curiously. "Where'd
you get those clothes?" he asked. "I don't know anybody

who has clothes like that. Are you from out West?"

"San Francisco?" a sandy-haired boy asked. "I heard they dress funny in San Francisco."

"No, I'm from . . ." Jack's voice trailed off. Where *was* he from, if not from Odyssey? "Near here," he finally said. He glanced away self-consciously and decided to change the subject. "Maybe you can help me," he said. "I'm looking for anyone who knows the pastor of the church that's—" Again he had to stop himself. He didn't know the name of the church or where it was.

"Must be Reverend Andrew you're talking about," the sandy-haired boy said helpfully. "He's rector of that church yonder." The boy pointed through a gap between the buildings to a church sitting about a hundred yards away in the middle of a parklike area. It looked peaceful in the afternoon sunlight.

Jack was astounded. It was the church all right. "We must've climbed out the back and run *away* from town," he muttered.

"Pardon?" the freckle-faced boy asked.

Jack shook his head. "Nothing," he said. "I just need to talk to someone about the church."

The sandy-haired boy asked, "Why don't you go over and talk to the reverend himself at the church?"

Obviously, whatever had happened in the church wasn't common knowledge around the town. "I'm not sure anyone's there," Jack said honestly.

"Then you'd better check the hotel," the freckle-faced

boy said. "The reverend stays there when he isn't at the church."

"At a hotel?"

"Yep. He's been living there ever since his house got burned down," the boy said.

"That's what he gets for fighting with the slave hunters," another boy interjected.

"Quiet, Jeb," the freckle-faced boy snapped, then pointed down the street. "Now, just go across the street there, and the hotel is on the end—at the corner."

"Thanks, guys."

"Guys?"

"Er, *friends*." With a quick nod to them, Jack dodged the horses and wagons that seemed to come from every direction on the street and made it to the other side. He looked back at the group of boys, who talked animatedly between themselves while they watched him. He waved and headed down the sidewalk.

The Odyssey Hotel sat at the corner of Main Street and McAlister. It looked familiar to Jack with its large, frosted windows embedded in richly carved doors. Then he remembered that he'd only seen pictures of it while he was on a school field trip to Odyssey's historical museum. Jack's feeling of being out of place was intensified when he also remembered that the hotel burned down in 1904 during Odyssey's great fire. It was like seeing the *Titanic* before it sailed.

Parallel to the hotel but on the other side of McAlister

Street sat City Hall, with its large, ornate clock tower. The huge face of the clock peered at him like an old friend. It was the only thing so far that Jack was certain he recognized, though the tower still had scaffolding along one side for workers to add some finishing touches. Jack searched his memory from that field trip. The clock tower was finished in . . . the fall of 1858. *That's now*, he thought with a smile. Mrs. Sexton, the museum guide, had said that it was completed around the same time that Big Ben was put into the tower at Westminster Palace in London. Folks in Odyssey were proud to share the experience with their foreign cousins.

Jack walked into the hotel and was immediately impressed by the marble and plush, red decoration of the lobby, tastefully matched by patterned wallpaper, shelves with Chinese-looking vases, flowers, and dark brown wood-work along the edges of the ceilings and floors. The entire reception desk was also dark brown wood. Camel-backed sofas, loveseats, and wing-backed chairs with frilly skirts were scattered around the room. An elegant staircase led away from the lobby and up to parts unknown. On the other side of a wide, curtained entryway just to the right of the stairs, Jack could see what looked like a restaurant or saloon. Somewhere inside, a piano player announced that he would play a new song and fumbled his way through "The Yellow Rose of Texas."

Men and women in varying styles of formal and casual clothes wandered around the lobby. Businessmen in smart suits chatted seriously in a corner. A man wearing a large, round hat and carrying a long, silver-headed cane plucked a gold watch from his waistcoat and checked the time. The women wore bell-shaped dresses that rustled as they walked past. Overburdened porters moved quickly about with their patrons' luggage in hand.

Jack stepped up to the reception desk, but a man with a thick mustache stepped in front of him and slapped a coin down on the counter. "This should take care of my room and any extras," he said quickly. He was obviously in a hurry.

The spectacled clerk eyed the small, gold coin warily. "Ah, I see," he said. "One of those new three-dollar pieces. It's the first one I've seen."

"Not sure they'll last," the man said simply. "Apply the difference to my account. I don't want to miss the train."

"Yes, Mr. Prentice," the clerk said, but the man was already on his way out the door.

Jack approached the counter and stood on the tips of his toes to get the clerk's attention. "Excuse me—"

"I'll be right with you, son," the clerk said as he turned his attention to shoving pieces of paper into a collection of cubbyholes on the wall behind him.

Jack waited patiently as bits of conversations around him drifted by. One man complained to a woman, "It just doesn't make sense that Minnesota can get the statehood and Kansas can't. I swear, you give those Washington politicians a new capitol to meet in and they lose their marbles."

"I'm telling you, Beck and Russell say Cherry Creek is

teeming with gold. I'm thinking of making the trip out myself," one traveler said to his companion on the way through the lobby.

His friend replied, "All the way to Colorado? That's clear on the other side of the Kansas Territory! It'll take a mighty long time to get there."

"Not so long these days," the first man countered. "The Overland Stage Coach made it from St. Louis to Los Angeles in 20 days!"

A lady sat in a corner chair reading a book. A younger girl eased down next to her and asked what she was reading. "*The Courtship of Miles Standish,* by Henry Wadsworth Longfellow," she said, holding it up proudly. "I just received it by post from New England!"

A man reading a newspaper suddenly laughed and said to his friend, "It's been over a month since the transatlantic cable stopped working, and now they aren't sure they'll ever get it fixed. I reckon President Buchanan and Queen Victoria won't be able to send messages across the Atlantic anymore."

His friend replied with a chuckle, "Not sure why anyone would *want* to send cables back and forth across the Atlantic."

A cheery, roly-poly fellow—obviously a salesman— entreated a bored-looking man about the "revolution" that the new "Mason Jar" would bring to the country. He was giving the man the chance to invest a small sum that he assured him would yield 10 times the amount later.

But the conversation that caught Jack's full attention was

between two wealthy-looking men nearby who spoke in hushed but agitated tones about a debate on slavery between Abraham Lincoln and someone named Stephen Douglas.

"I'm tired to death of hearing about it," the first man said. "Let the politicians decide and be done with it."

The second man shook his head. "I don't think this is a matter to be legislated," he said. "People like John Brown and those abolitionists won't let it lie. The way it's going, I figure there's going to be fighting."

"A war?"

"God forbid," the man said. "But you see how it's tearing Odyssey apart. If that's any indication of the mood in the rest of the country . . . well, I can't predict what'll happen."

Someone loudly cleared his throat. Jack realized it was the hotel clerk. "You wanted something, young man?" he said.

"I'm looking for Reverend Andrew. He lives here, right?" Jack answered.

"He does, but he isn't here at the moment. Did you look for him at the church? That's where he generally is at this time of day."

Suddenly a man rushed in through the door. He called out breathlessly, "Has anyone seen the sheriff?"

"Not here. Why? What's wrong, Albert?" the clerk asked.

"We've got another *incident* behind the church!" he replied.

There was a flurry of activity as some of the men reacted and ran to Albert, then squeezed out the door.

The clerk groaned, "Not another one."

"Incident?" Jack asked.

"Yep." The clerk frowned at Jack. "That'll probably be Reverend Andrew's doing. Reckon you'll find him wherever that crowd's going."

Jack sped out the door after the men.

CHAPTER SEVEN

Matt and the girl sat under an elm tree near the cemetery. Normally, Matt might've thought what a beautiful day it was to sit under an elm tree, with the birds chirping happily and the yellow and brown leaves falling gently. It was another gorgeous fall day in Odyssey, only it wasn't his Odyssey, and the edge of danger cut through the pretty picture like a razor blade.

"What's your name?" Matt suddenly asked.

She had been staring wearily at the tombstones and answered so softly that Matt barely heard her: "Eveline."

"Eveline who?"

"Not Eveline *who.* Just Eveline."

"Don't you have a last name?"

"I think we did once, but I don't remember what it was."

They sat in silence again while Matt tried to grasp the notion of a girl who didn't know her own last name. It made him uncomfortable. He knew a little about slavery from his classes at school and some of the books he had read. But this was the real thing. He didn't like it. He squirmed impatiently. What was taking Jack so long? he wondered. Where was Eveline's father? Did he get away from the men in the tunnel? *I sure hope so,* he thought. *Otherwise, I don't know what we're going to do.*

"Can you read?" Eveline asked.

"Sure I can read," he replied, surprised by the question.

"So can I," Eveline said with a big smile.

"That's what you said before." Matt shrugged and couldn't figure out why it was so important to her. "Everybody I know can read."

She looked at him carefully, as if trying to decide whether he was teasing her. "Everybody? Even folks of color?" she asked.

"Yeah. What's the big deal? You go to school, and they teach you to read."

"You went to *school?*" she asked, awed.

"Of course I did, er—*do,*" Matt said. He was getting a little irritated with this game. "Don't you go to school?"

Eveline shook her head. "Huh uh. Slaves aren't allowed to go to school. Our masters don't want us to learn nothing but the work we do. That's why I had to learn to read in secret. Aunt Tabby taught me how, but she said I wasn't ever supposed to let white folks know or they might put me in jail or hurt me."

"Put you in jail for knowing how to read?" Matt nearly shouted. "That's crazy! Why would anybody do that?"

"Aunt Tabby said they don't want us to read because it gives us ideas," she said.

Matt didn't know how to react. He remembered from history class that most slaves couldn't read, but it never occurred to him that they weren't *allowed* to read.

The distinct sound of horses' hooves beating the road worked its way through the air. Then came the sound of the churning of wagon wheels. Matt stood up to look. "Somebody's coming," he said and turned to Eveline, but she was gone. He was amazed by how quickly she had disappeared. "Eveline?" He looked around for her. She was a few yards away, waving at him from behind a large tombstone. "What are you doing?"

She waved frantically at him.

Torn between running to the road for help or going to her, he hesitated for a moment. She waved with greater agitation, and he decided to find out what her problem was first. "What's wrong?" he asked. "Maybe it's your father."

"And maybe it's the slave hunters!" she whispered. "We have to hide until we can be sure."

Matt knew instantly that she was right. He didn't have much to fear in his world, but in *her* world, there was plenty to be afraid of. He ducked behind the tombstone with her and watched the road.

First came a man on horseback. Matt thought it might've been one of the men in the tunnel, but he couldn't be sure. Following behind him, another horse pulled a wooden wagon with two men sitting up front. Matt still couldn't be sure whether they were slave hunters—how could he?—until Eveline gasped and pointed. Tied up in the back of the wagon, beaten and bloody, was Eveline's father. She made as if she might rush out to him, but Matt grabbed her arm. They didn't breathe as the wagon drifted past. Curls of dust were kicked up by the horses and wheels.

"They got my daddy," she moaned. "They're gonna take him back!"

Matt didn't know what to say or do. "Maybe when Jack comes back with the reverend, we can—"

"No! I have to follow them. I don't wanna lose my daddy!" With that, she took off before Matt could stop her.

"Wait! You'll get caught!" he whispered as loudly as he dared.

"Freedom's no good without my daddy," Eveline snapped back, then weaved her way quickly through the graveyard as the wagon disappeared around the bend.

Matt leaned against the cold, damp tombstone and groaned. What was he supposed to do? He glanced hopefully up the road, praying that Jack, the reverend, and a posse of good guys might be following the slave hunters to rescue Clarence and keep Matt from having to make a decision. A rabbit scurried out to the center of the road, then dashed on to the other side. That was all.

Matt couldn't see Eveline anymore. What was he supposed to do? But he knew there was only one answer.

He couldn't let Eveline follow the slave hunters alone.

CHAPTER EIGHT

A crowd of men had gathered in a grove of trees not far from the church. Jack rushed up anxiously and maneuvered so he could see what had happened. A man knelt next to a tree—to cut the ropes that held Reverend Andrew. A small ribbon of blood slid down the side of Andrew's face. Jack's heart pounded furiously as he looked all around for Clarence. He wasn't there.

Reverend Andrew climbed to his feet and, in a voice filled with anger, told the crowd what had happened. "They burst into the church, grabbed us, and dragged us here. They tied me up and proceeded to beat the poor slave mercilessly. They wanted to know where his daughter was, but he wouldn't tell them. That made them even angrier, so they beat him more. I protested until they gagged me. They tied me here and hauled the slave off."

"What was a runaway doing in your church, Reverend?" one man asked with undisguised annoyance. "You're not part of that there Underground Railroad, are you?"

"What do you mean by the question, sir?" another man answered. "If the church can't be a haven to *all* men in *all* conditions, then what's it for?"

"I'd better run home and check my fences then," the first man sneered. "What'll become of my business when my cows and pigs know they need only run away to the church for protection?"

A few men snickered at this remark.

"You go too far, Thomas," a man snapped back. "We're talking about *men,* not animals!"

"Are we?" the sneering man replied.

"Yes, we are!"

The reverend held up his hands in appeal to the men. "This isn't the time or place for a debate," he said. "I ask only that the men here who abhor the practice of these slave hunters come with me. We must rescue the poor unfortunate who is even now being unwillingly taken back to the South!"

Half the men murmured their consent, while the sneering man and his group grunted and turned away. One muttered something about the reverend getting what he deserved for helping runaways.

After the men had gone, Reverend Andrew gathered the remainder around him. "My guess is they took the Connellsville Road," he told them. "But there's a girl—the runaway's daughter—who is hiding somewhere in the region. We must scour the area and find her lest she fall into their hands as well!"

With this, Jack stepped forward. "Excuse me, Reverend, but—"

At the sight of Jack, Andrew's eyes grew wide. "You! You were in the church!"

"Yes, sir. I know where the girl is. She's with my friend just a couple of miles from here. I came back to find you to—"

"You know where she is? Excellent!" Andrew exclaimed, then turned to the crowd. "Get your horses and wagons, and meet me at the church. God help us to stop this horrendous deed!"

With roars of approval, the crowd scattered. Reverend Andrew put his hand on Jack's shoulder. "Well done, son," he said. "What's your name?"

"Jack," he replied.

"It's providential that you came when you did," he said. "Where is the girl and your friend?"

"At a cemetery a couple of miles from here. The girl said it's where her dad would meet her."

"Clarence was a smart man to prearrange a meeting place if anything went wrong. Which cemetery? Odyssey has several."

Jack frowned. He had no idea *which* cemetery it was. Then he remembered: "The girl said that diseased people are buried there."

"I know the graveyard," the reverend said with a nod. "Now I need to impose on you further. Run as hard as you can to the girl and your friend, and keep them hidden until I arrive with help. Trust no one. Clarence didn't tell the slave hunters where his daughter was, but they might be searching for her. Now *go,* lad!"

The sun was going down by the time Jack reached the graveyard. His side hurt from all the running, and he couldn't remember a time when he felt more tired. "Matt?" he called out. "It's me—Jack!"

Silence.

"Don't mess around, Matt," Jack called out again. A cool breeze blew past, and his skin went goose-pimply. Something was wrong. He crept around the tombstones and wooden grave markers, hoping Matt and the girl really were just teasing him. He then widened his search to include the surrounding woods up to the road. No sign of them.

"Where are you?" he eventually shouted with exasperation.

His voice echoed and came back to him empty.

With no better ideas, Jack slumped down next to a tree by the road. All he could do was wait for Reverend Andrew.

CHAPTER NINE

With the sound of thunder, the reverend and about 20 men arrived at the cemetery just as the sun ducked below the horizon. They carried rifles and blazing torches. Jack, with obvious relief, ran out to the road to meet them.

"Well?" Andrew called as he leapt off his horse.

"They're not here," Jack said.

"Are you sure?" a man with thick whiskers asked. Then he signaled for some of the men to fan out and search.

"Believe me! I already checked," Jack said. "They aren't here."

"That's enough for me," another man shouted. "Let's go after those blasted slave hunters and show 'em we don't tolerate this kind of thing in Odyssey."

The men shouted their approval and were yanking at the reins of their horses when another posse raced up and surrounded them. Curses and insults were exchanged between the two groups, and Jack was afraid a fight might break out.

"Hold on, boys," a lean man shouted from the front of the group as he reined his horse to a stop. He had a star pinned to his gray flannel shirt. "Just what in tarnation do you think you're doing?"

"Slave hunters again, Sheriff. Nabbed a runaway slave and probably his daughter."

"Sorry, boys, but the law says the slave hunters can take runaways back to their masters. Nothing you or me can do about that."

"We'll show you what we can do about it!" a large man shouted.

"Whoa now! I won't have it!" the sheriff insisted. "Not in my territory. You go after those slave hunters and sure as I'm sitting here, there'll be a fight. Somebody'll get hurt or killed. So just put your guns away and go home. No point getting worked up over somebody else's problem. These slaves aren't our business."

"But my friend might be with them—and he wasn't a slave!" Jack called out.

The sheriff jerked his head around to look at Jack. His eyes narrowed. "What are you talking about?" he demanded. "Are you saying they kidnapped somebody?"

Jack shuffled uneasily. "We think they took him."

"Well, I'll be doggoned. Not like them to be kidnapping white boys," the sheriff said.

"Matt isn't white," Jack said.

"But he's free," Reverend Andrew interjected.

"Matt? I don't remember a free black Negro named Matt registering at my office."

Jack was surprised. "Register at your office? Why would he have to do that?"

"For his own sake. Free blacks are supposed to register so the slave hunters won't have a right to capture them. Everybody knows that." The sheriff leaned forward on the front of his saddle. "Did he do that?"

"No," Jack said. "We didn't know he was supposed to. I mean, where we come from, you don't—"

"That's all that can be done then," the sheriff announced. He turned his attention to the crowd of men. "Now, I'm going to ask you all *nicely* to go home and forget about this thing. I won't have a pack of vigilantes riding across the country-side shooting or getting shot by the slave hunters. You can go home or spend the night in jail. It's up to you."

For a tense moment, the sheriff stared down the reverend's posse until, one by one, they yanked their reins and spun their horses toward Odyssey. Reverend Andrew stood alone with Jack.

"Well, Reverend?" the sheriff asked.

"Have it your way, Sheriff," Andrew said in a cold tone.

The sheriff sighed heavily. "I don't like this business, you know. I don't like it at all." He loudly clicked his tongue and spurred his horse away. With various grunts and "yahs!" his men followed, leaving a cloud of dust to coat Jack and the reverend.

"That's it?" Jack asked with disbelief. "We're just supposed to sit back and let the slave hunters take Matt?"

Reverend Andrew put his hand on Jack's shoulder. "This thing isn't over yet," he said with determination.

CHAPTER TEN

Matt and Eveline crawled beneath a thick bush and watched the clearing where the slave hunters had set up camp for the night. The hunters had tied their horses to the buckboard wagon's wheels, gathered wood for a fire, and pulled out a tin pot to make what smelled to Matt like meat broth. It made his stomach ache for the food. That's what he wanted more than anything, he thought: to be home for a hot meal and to sleep in his own bed.

The thick, brown forest dirt under the tangled branches of the bush was moist and cold. Matt cradled his head in his arms and closed his eyes.

They'd followed the slave hunters for miles. How many miles, Matt didn't know. It was all he could do just to keep up with Eveline, whose speed and energy seemed without limit. *How did I get into this,* he kept asking himself, *and how do I get out of it?* He clung to the hope that Jack was not far behind them with Reverend Andrew or, better yet, Mr.

Whittaker. Matt was sorry he'd ever laid eyes on The Imagination Station.

"There's my daddy." Eveline whispered so softly that, again, Matt almost didn't hear her. He lifted his head and looked. She pointed to an enormous oak tree in the shadows on the edge of the clearing. Clarence was tied tightly to it. He hung his head. Matt couldn't tell if he was sleeping or just too exhausted to sit up straight.

The three slave hunters fixed their meal silently and seemed to be listening for anything unusual in the woods. Matt guessed they were worried that someone from Odyssey might follow them. Little could they know they were right. But they were expecting men and horses, not two kids hiding under a bush.

"I don't think anyone's coming," one of the slave hunters said.

For the first time, Matt was able to take a hard look at the men. The one who just spoke was tall and wiry, with a bushy mustache perched under a hooked nose. Even in the firelight, Matt could see he had a dangerous-looking face, with deep lines going every which way like a road map. He had long, thinning, gray hair that sprayed out from under an old, weather-beaten cowboy hat. Eventually Matt picked up that he was named Hank.

"I didn't believe they would. The sheriff would see to that," said a round-faced, clean-shaven man in a bowler hat named Sonny. He pulled a pipe from his waistcoat pocket—its buttons stretched to their limit by his bulk—and settled back against a rock.

The third man was the one Matt was sure he had seen in the basement at Whit's End. He had squinty eyes that looked as if someone had drawn two quarter moons above his cheeks. Thick eyebrows crowned them and splayed out like birds' wings. His face was lean and looked even longer by the way his mouth pushed downward in a permanent frown. He was the boss, which was obvious only because it was what the other two men called him. He grabbed the coffee pot from the fire and poured himself a cup. "We need to take shifts to make sure nobody sneaks up on us tonight," he said in a hoarse, scratchy voice.

Matt took in the scene and couldn't imagine how to help Clarence. He thought he might be able to sneak around and untie his ropes. But then what? The three slave hunters would quickly catch them again. *What are we going to do?* he wondered.

"You wanna give the chattel some of this soup?" Hank asked.

Boss glanced over at Clarence, then shook his head. "Not sure I'm interested in wasting any good food on him after the trouble he's caused us."

"You call this good?" Sonny grimaced and threw his tin down playfully.

Hank sniffed indignantly, "You're welcome to eat something else if you have a better offer."

"Let's just get to Huntsville and we'll have all the offers we want," Boss said with a chuckle.

"So long as our buck here gets us the reward money we want," Sonny said.

"How 'bout that, Boss?" Hank asked.

Boss scrubbed his prickly chin and stood up. "Not gonna fetch as much as we expected without the daughter." He walked over and kicked Clarence's leg.

Clarence stirred and slowly lifted his head with a groan.

Boss kicked him again. "You've robbed us, boy," he said. "We were supposed to get you and your daughter, and you helped her get away. You're gonna have to pay us the difference—or I reckon you'll have to be punished somehow."

"You wanna punish him? Give him some of the soup," Sonny said.

"You want some soup?" Boss asked Clarence. As if on cue, Hank walked over with a tin of the soup and knelt next to the bound man. "You must be hungry after such a long trip."

Hank held the tin of soup up to Clarence's mouth. Clarence looked as if he didn't want it.

"Go on, take some," Hank said.

Clarence turned his head away.

"Can't you hear, boy? He said to *take some soup*." Boss kicked Clarence harder.

Clarence shook his head. "No, thank you, sir," he said. "I'm not hungry."

"What? That's not the point. We want you to eat. We want you to be a big, strong buck for your master when we march you in. *Now eat!*"

Hank kicked at Clarence.

"Daddy!" Eveline gasped.

Every muscle in Matt's body tensed as the two men taunted and kicked at Clarence. Sonny sat nearby and laughed at the scene. Matt knew they had to do something, but he couldn't think what. Then he wondered, *What if we could create a diversion?* If he could get the slave hunters away from Clarence, Eveline could untie her father. He turned to Eveline to tell her the plan but didn't get the chance. She scrambled out from under the bushes and raced into the clearing.

"Not again!" Matt groaned to himself.

"Stop it! Stop doing that to my daddy!" Eveline cried.

The two men, startled by the girl's sudden appearance, swung around. Sonny dropped his pipe.

"No, child!" Clarence shouted as he strained at the ropes.

Hank let out a bark of a laugh. "Well, as I live and breathe!" he said. "Look, Boss, it's the girl."

"I see her," Boss replied. "What are you doing here, my little pickaninny?" he asked Eveline. "Come to help your daddy?"

Eveline stood frozen where she was, but her eyes moved quickly from man to man in case one made a move for her.

"Eveline," Clarence croaked.

"You want me to grab her?" Hank asked.

"Shut up," Boss snapped. Then he smiled at Eveline and asked, "You wanna help your daddy, *Eveline?* Then give me your hand. Come with us. It'll help him more than anything else you can do."

Matt realized this was as much of a diversion as he could have planned himself. He crawled backward, keeping out of sight behind the bush, and then rushed around the edge of the clearing toward the tree to which Clarence was tied. He knew he had little time and ran as fast and as quietly as he could.

"Come on, Eveline," he heard Boss say.

Through the limbs of the trees, he saw Eveline standing perfectly still by the firelight. Her eyes still darted like a rabbit's who'd been surrounded by wolves. But they also betrayed that she had acted on impulse and didn't know what to do next.

"Run, child!" Clarence shouted. "Don't let 'em take you. *Run!*"

Matt was now behind the tree and at the ropes holding Clarence. He peered around and saw Eveline shuffle anxiously. She was stricken by indecision. Boss took a step toward her. "Come on, girl," he said.

In the darkness of the woods, Matt had a hard time seeing the ropes. He felt around for the knots and, with a sinking heart, realized they weren't there. They must be on the other side, with Clarence.

"Don't listen to him, Eveline," Clarence commanded his daughter. "You run now, you hear? Don't let him get any closer! Run!"

The words somehow got through, and with a last, despairing look, she tore away just as Boss dove for her. Gazellelike, she bounded into the dark woods.

"Get her!" Boss yelled. The three men disappeared into the darkness after her.

Matt's mind reeled as he tried to think. How could he get Clarence untied? Peeking around to make sure everyone had gone, he circled the tree to Clarence.

"What are you doing here?" Clarence asked him, amazed. "Are you crazy?"

"We're here to rescue you!" Matt announced.

"Rescue me? Oh, son, you *are* crazy."

"How can I get you free?" Matt asked as he tugged at the ropes.

Clarence looked around frantically and said, "You'll never get these knots undone. A knife. Look around the wagon for a knife."

Matt ran to the wagon and searched through the bedrolls, saddlebags, and a crate filled with ropes, tools, and tarp. No knife. In a harsh whisper, he called back to Clarence, "I can't find it. Are you sure there's a knife here?"

"Watch out!" Clarence shouted, looking beyond Matt.

Matt heard a low chuckle behind him and turned.

CHAPTER ELEVEN

M an alive, this beats the dutch!" Hank wheezed happily as he secured the ropes on Matt's and Eveline's wrists. "Good thing you came along, Wylie."

"I guess it was," Wylie replied. Matt stared at him with all the hatred he could muster. He recognized Wylie as the black man who had arrived in the tunnel right after Matt and Jack. Clarence had accused him of pretending to be a slave in order to catch runaways. Clarence was right.

"You're gonna get it for tying me up like this," Matt fumed.

"Shut up," Hank hissed in Matt's ear.

"I figure you can add this boy to what you owe me. You have *three* to take back with you now," Wylie said with a smile.

"That wasn't part of the deal," Boss said.

"Neither was you going so far out. We were supposed to

meet in Gower's field, you'll recall. All this riding hurts my hindparts," Wylie complained. "So just add a few dollars to what you owe me."

Boss looked as if he might argue, then changed his mind. "I swear, I've never known a darky to haggle the way you do. But you do good work, and I won't begrudge you that." Boss marched over to his saddlebag and pulled out a small pouch. Coins clinked as he poured them into his palm, counting carefully as he did. When he was satisfied with the amount, he held out his hand to Wylie. "What we agreed and then some."

Wylie took the money. "Pleasure doing business with you."

"You oughtta be ashamed of yourself," Clarence growled at Wylie. "Betraying your own people for 30 pieces of silver. You're a *Judas.* You sold yourself to the devil."

Wylie chuckled in response. "I'll be thinking about you when I have a hot bath and good meal in Connellsville tonight," he said. He tipped his hat to the three slave hunters. "Good hunting, my friends. You know where to find me if you need me again!" He bowed, then made his way into the woods.

"I never liked him and never liked doing business with him," Sonny said. "I hope you didn't give him much. Do you think this boy'll fetch a good price?"

Boss grunted, "We'll get what we expected for the buck and his girl, but this one's scrawny." He nudged Matt with the edge of his boot.

"You do anything to me and you'll be in *big* trouble," Matt challenged.

Hank and Sonny laughed at the boy's spirit. Boss didn't. He squinted at Matt thoughtfully. "Strange. He doesn't act like a slave," he said.

"I'm *not* a slave!" Matt shouted.

"Then I reckon you better explain yourself," Boss said. "Where're you from, and what're you doing here?"

Matt sat up proudly and said, "I'm from Odyssey."

"Are you?" Boss said skeptically. "You sure don't dress like anybody I've ever seen in Odyssey. Where'd you get those funny-looking clothes?" He tugged at Matt's jacket and sweatshirt.

"Well, I'm not from the Odyssey you know but from a different Odyssey—one in the future."

The slave hunters looked at each other, bewildered. "What in blazes are you talking about?" Boss asked.

"See, Jack and I went through the tunnel to the workroom in Whit's End, and that's where we found The Imagination Station."

"Whit's End?" Boss shook his head.

"Crazy as a loon," Sonny mumbled.

Matt protested, "I'm serious! We got into The Imagination Station, and the next thing we knew, we were in the tunnel again, but it wasn't the tunnel leading to Whit's End, but to the church where we saw Reverend Andrew—"

"What a yarn!" Hank said with a chuckle.

"I'm telling the truth!" Matt shouted.

Boss nudged him harder with the toe of his boot. "Listen, boy," he said, "I wasn't born in the woods to be scared by an owl—or to have a little urchin cut shines with me."

"Huh?"

"Do you have papers? I need to see some proof that you're free," Boss demanded.

"We don't need papers where I come from!" Matt said.

"I reckon that's too bad for you," Boss said. He turned to tell his companions, "Looks like he goes with us."

Matt squirmed. "I don't know who you guys think you are, but you're going to be arrested for kidnapping if you don't let us go *right now!* I mean it. Mr. Whittaker is going to show up any minute, and the police are going to lock you up and throw away the key!"

"Shut up, boy," Boss said.

"No, I *won't* shut up! You have no right to tie us up and—"

Matt didn't get to finish his sentence. Boss suddenly backhanded him across the face. "I said to *shut up*, and that's what I meant!"

Matt was so startled that at first he didn't notice the pain in the side of his face like a bee sting or the tear that slid down his cheek without permission.

"All right, boys, let's get some shut-eye," Boss said. "Tomorrow we take to the river. You're on the first watch, Sonny."

"Me?" Sonny complained.

"Yeah, you. Then me. Then Hank."

After the men were settled down for the night, Eveline

leaned over to Matt. "Are you all right?" she whispered.

Matt swallowed back his tears and nodded.

"Don't you fret," Eveline said soothingly. "You'll get used to it. That's how they treat us."

Matt thought, *No, I won't. I'll* never *get used to it.*

CHAPTER TWELVE

R everend Andrew lived in a modest two-bedroom apartment in the Odyssey Hotel. To Jack, it looked the way rooms did in Western movies. Andrew had assembled a makeshift study on one side of the room, with a rolltop desk, shelves overburdened with books, a small sofa and reading chair, and an end table with a kerosene lamp. All of it sat atop a large, patterned throw rug that covered most of the wooden flooring. Small, painted pictures of country hills hung at odd angles on the walls.

At the moment, Jack and Andrew were sitting on the opposite side of the room at the dining table. Since he didn't have a stove on which to cook, Reverend Andrew had brought up a meal of beef and potatoes from the hotel restaurant.

"No doubt you're wondering why I'm living in the hotel," Andrew said as he chomped on a particularly chewy piece of beef. "The apartment was given to me by some of our parishioners after slave hunters burned down my house several years ago."

"They burned down your *house?*" Jack asked, vaguely remembering that the boys on the street had mentioned the fact. That conversation seemed like such a long time ago.

"It was the rectory not far from the church. Perhaps you saw what's left of it today," Andrew said.

Jack nodded as he remembered the shell of the house near the woods. "But why did they burn down your house?" he asked.

Reverend Andrew shook his head. "It's a long story. They didn't appreciate the way I helped a family of runaways. The house caught fire when the fools decided to smoke the family out of the tunnel. That incident secured my place in the abolitionist movement. If I doubted the importance of the Underground Railroad before, I didn't afterward. I've dedicated all I have to helping where I can to stop this abomination before God."

Jack frowned. "I don't understand how people can treat other people that way—just because of the color of their skin."

"Obviously I agree," Reverend Andrew said. "The Scriptures are clear about the dignity of all those for whom the Son of God died—regardless of their color. Slavery makes a sham of our humanity, a lie of our place as a Christian nation. The love of Christ cannot be spoken of with our mouths while our hands whip the backs of our brothers and shackle their arms and legs. God must weep in heaven. He must!"

Jack sat up, captivated by the power of Andrew's words.

But Andrew didn't continue. He simply sighed, "In many ways, it's worse now than it ever was. The debates have certainly stirred things up."

"Debates?"

"You don't know? Where have you been, lad? I thought everyone knew about the Douglas-Lincoln debates."

Jack thought of the snippet of conversation he'd heard in the hotel lobby that afternoon. "Oh, yeah. But why is everyone so upset about a debate between Abraham Lincoln and that other guy? Or is it because Lincoln is president and—"

"*President* Lincoln?" Reverend Andrew bellowed. "I hardly think he's likely to ever become president. Not now. Not after taking such a hard stand on slavery. I'm all for him, of course, but I can't imagine the majority of other people are. Douglas will probably win because of his confounded stand on states' rights."

Jack shook his head. None of it made sense to him, and he said so.

Reverend Andrew leaned back and spoke patiently. "Senator Stephen Douglas and Abraham Lincoln recently conducted a series of debates about the issue of slavery. It is Lincoln's intention to be the next Republican senator from Illinois. You see, he caused quite a stir earlier in the year when he made a speech at the Republican convention. He said that a 'house divided against itself cannot stand. . . . I believe this government cannot endure permanently half slave and half free.' I'll never forget those words—an echo of the very sentiments of Christ." He paused for a moment in a reverent silence.

Jack took another bite of his beef. It was tough and stringy.

Reverend Andrew continued. "Douglas, a Democrat, argued that democracy itself was at stake if states—and the new territories in the West—aren't allowed to decide the issue of slavery for themselves. He was quite eloquent. So was Lincoln. And by the end of the debates, Lincoln laid his cards on the table. He turned the subject of slavery from a political issue to a *moral* one. He has appealed to the whole nation to reject slavery as an institution."

"And he's right!" Jack said.

"He is, indeed," Andrew said soberly. "And though the nation may not accept his message, *I* certainly do. Which is why I won't let those slave hunters get away with taking Clarence, Eveline, and your friend. I've never lost a runaway. I'm not about to lose any now."

Jack bit into a potato. He was surprised by how plain it tasted but didn't want to offend Andrew by saying so. "But how will we get them back?" he asked.

"Ah! I have a most clever plan, if I may say so myself," the reverend said with a smile.

"What are we going to do?"

Andrew frowned. "We? I'm sorry, lad, but it's a bit too risky for you to help out."

"But Matt is *my* friend. I *have* to be allowed to help!"

Jack exclaimed, nearly spilling his glass of water.

Reverend Andrew rubbed his chin thoughtfully for a moment. "An assistant would be helpful," he said, "but I need you to tell me who your parents are so I can speak to them about it."

Jack grimaced. "I can tell you who my parents are, but you won't be able to find them."

"Won't I?"

"No, sir." Jack poked at the last of the potato with his fork as he tried to decide how to tell Reverend Andrew the truth. He realized he couldn't. The truth sounded ridiculous, even to his own mind. Who would believe that he had been transported from the future by a machine called The Imagination Station that some inventor named Whit had created? Jack sure wouldn't.

"Are you an orphan?" the reverend asked gently.

Jack mused on the question. In a way, he and Matt *were* orphans since, technically speaking, their parents hadn't even been born yet. "Something like that," Jack replied non-committally.

"Then I'll assume you have nowhere to stay tonight."

"No, sir, I don't."

"You do now. I have a guest room for just such occasions. It has a feather bed—not straw. I believe you'll find it comfortable. I'll put some fresh water in your washbasin so you can clean up before you go to sleep." The reverend stood up as a signal that it was time to call it a night.

"But . . . what about the plan?" Jack asked as he also

stood up.

"In due course, lad," Andrew said. "We'll have plenty of time on the train journey to Huntsville to talk it through."

"Huntsville?"

"It's in Alabama. I'm sure that's where the slave hunters are taking Clarence and Eveline."

"How do you know that?"

"Because it's where Clarence's master lives." Reverend Andrew began clearing up the dishes. "Now, if you need anything at all, simply let me know."

Jack hesitated for a moment. Andrew looked at him quizzically. Jack cleared his throat. "Well . . . I was wondering where the bathroom is."

"There's one on the second floor. But it's terribly late to order a bath," Andrew said.

"Actually, I don't need to order a *bath*. I need to *use* the bathroom."

Reverend Andrew look at him, perplexed.

"You know, the bathroom? The *toilet?*"

Suddenly the reverend's face lit up. "Oh, I see! The *necessary*. You want to use the chamber pot!"

Jack shrugged. "Whatever you call it."

"Certainly! Why did you have to ask? It's where you would expect it to be."

Jack shuffled uneasily. "And . . . uh . . . where would I expect it to be?"

"Under your bed, of course," Andrew said, giving Jack an odd look. "Now, go on, first door on the left. Make yourself at home."

"Right," Jack muttered as he walked down the small hallway. "Make myself at home."

CHAPTER THIRTEEN

At dawn the next morning, Matt, Clarence, and Eveline were virtually thrown into the back of the wagon by Hank and Sonny. Still tied up, they bounced along dirt roads that led them four hours later to an old cabin somewhere along the Mississippi River. A toothless old woman leered at them as Boss paid her to hire a flatboat. They haggled over the price, but there was a playfulness to it that made Matt think the two were old friends. Matt suspected that Boss and the old woman had done business to transport slaves many times before.

Sonny slapped the reins, and the horse drew the wagon down a potholed path to a small dock on the river. The sound of the rippling water normally would have brought Matt pleasure. Today, it filled him with fear. He knew that once they were away from shore, Jack would never be able to find him.

Hank gruffly pushed the three of them off the wagon and

guided them to a large, raftlike boat at the end of the dock. It was the flatboat, or "ark." Matt didn't have to guess about how it got its name. The flatboat had a shelter in the center for passengers or cargo. Matt considered jumping over the side, but he realized he wouldn't get far (except to the bottom of the river) with his hands tied.

Hank shoved them into the cabin of the boat. "Get down there next to those crates," he barked. The three prisoners obliged, sitting down in what looked like a mix of straw, dirt, and seeping river water.

Another man appeared—scowling and shriveled beneath a sailor's cap. He spat a wad of tobacco into the corner. "I'm captain of this vessel," he announced, "and I don't want to hear a word out of any of you. No shouting, no talking, no singing. Not a peep. Can't stand the sound of you." He spat again.

"But I have to go to the bathroom," Matt said.

The captain looked at him a moment as if he needed to translate the words. Then he frowned. "I don't care!" he said as he stomped out and slammed the small door behind him.

The cabin had windows, but they were closed off by hinged boards. The air was sickly cold, with a smell that reminded Matt of a backed-up sewer. He looked helplessly at Clarence and Eveline, wondering if they were as scared as he was. If they were, they didn't show it. Clarence leaned back against the crate and closed his eyes. Eveline simply drew her knees up under her chin and rocked back and forth.

Matt felt something nudge against his foot. He looked

down in time to see a large, gray rat scamper by. He screamed.

****

They spent three days on the boat. Or was it four? Matt couldn't be certain. The boarded-up portholes of the cabin kept daylight to a minimum, and Matt couldn't tell anymore. A storm that turned the day into night threw his internal clock completely off.

They were a tiny vessel on a large river of mud and monstrous logs with tangled roots that stuck out like matted hair. Sometimes the flatboat would bump into the floating trees with a hard thump. Matt was certain that sooner or later, they'd hit something that would send them to the bottom.

Except when they were allowed out of the cabin for exercise and a meal of water, bread, or a suspicious-looking fish concoction, Matt's routine was to lie on the floor, kick at the rats, scratch at the fleas, and pray that somehow, some way, Jack or Mr. Whittaker would rescue him. A couple of times he tried to talk to Clarence and Eveline, but they shook their heads. "Those slave hunters'll whip you something awful," Clarence dared to whisper. "Just keep your mouth shut."

Once in a while, Matt heard the splash and patter of a steamboat's paddlewheel. The captain almost always hailed somebody on the riverboat—maybe the captain or a crewman—who'd respond with a quick toot of a whistle. It gave Matt hope. *There are people out there,* he remembered. *Somebody will rescue me.*

One afternoon when they'd all gathered on deck to eat, a steamboat passed by. Matt stared at it open-mouthed. It was like a long, trim palace on the water, with two fanciful chimneys, a large, glass-encased pilot house, and vast decks with people milling around happily behind white, ornate railings. The paddlewheels were enclosed in painted coverings that depicted a scene taken from the river itself: a wide expanse of water with a shoreline of thick forests and, in the center, a lonely, green island.

Matt watched the people on deck and wished that one might look at him. He prayed that somehow he could let them know he wasn't a slave and didn't belong on this awful boat. It took every ounce of strength and willpower to keep from shouting at the top of his lungs for help. But he knew that if he did that, Boss would do more than just backhand him.

Late that night, Matt was awakened by the frantic clamoring of a distant bell followed by a loud explosion. His heart pounded furiously as he heard people screaming. Something terrible had happened, he knew. The slave hunters stomped around the deck of the flatboat, shouting to each other. The captain commanded them to help him get the boat away. They must have succeeded, since the night drifted back to the river's normal sounds of water and frogs singing on the shore.

The next morning, Hank told them a riverboat had

collided with a massive collection of floating debris—trees, roots, and mud—and blown up. When Matt reacted with shock, Hank laughed at him. "Guess you don't know much about riverboats, do you, boy?" he said. "They blow up all the time."

The hours and minutes drifted by endlessly, like the river they rode upon. *Forever,* Matt thought as he slipped into despair again. *I'll be trapped here forever.* He thought of his parents and brother and sister who must be worried about him. Maybe they had even called the police by now. Would they think to look in Whit's workroom? Did the machine have some way of letting Whit know two boys had gone inside and turned it on? Matt turned these questions over and over in his mind. But he didn't know the answers.

Early one morning, Clarence sat up and muttered, "Must be Columbus."

Matt also sat up, wondering why Clarence mentioned the explorer's name until he heard the noise. Actually, it was a mixture of noises: horses' hooves on stone, rolling wagon wheels, shouts of hellos, barks of commands, a clanging bell, splashing water, wood banging upon wood—it was the noise of activity. Matt crawled expectantly onto his knees as the captain brought the boat to a halt by thumping it against a landing dock. Sonny threw open the cabin door and told the three prisoners to come out on deck.

"Columbus, Kentucky," the captain called out as if it were his duty to announce to the people on board where they were.

"We know, you old fool," Boss replied. "Now drop us off and be on your way." He sounded harsh, but then he clasped the captain's hand affectionately in his and thanked him for the service.

Matt glanced around. The town sat on a flat and marshy stretch of land circled by sickly looking trees. Half-houses were built along the dock area next to square buildings with shops. The streets bustled with merchants, customers, and travelers. Clerks sat in wooden chairs, tilted back against the wall, snoozing under their hats until a customer brought them awake. Pigs made feasts of watermelon rinds near the porches. Freight piles and skids littered the crumbling, stone wharf.

Boss had made arrangements for another wagon and two horses to be brought to the boat. The three prisoners were put straight onto the wagon and, with a loud "Yah!" from Hank, taken away. No one around the busy dock seemed to notice that a man and two kids were tied up like animals. Sadly, Matt realized that other blacks were doing the majority of work, lugging freight on and off the boats in chains, wearing rags.

Don't fret. You'll get used to it. That's what Eveline had said. Matt clenched his teeth and fought the resignation that wanted to lay claim to his heart. This nightmare would end, he knew. Somehow it would end.

CHAPTER FOURTEEN

T he old wagon rattled along the rutted roads across the southwestern tip of Kentucky, with its low plains and thick forests of oak and hickory. Their travel in the wagon was painfully slow compared to the speed of the cars Matt was used to. He began to wish they'd just hurry and get to where they were going—*anything* had to be better than the tediousness of the journey itself.

As they drove deeper into slave territory, Boss, Hank, and Sonny seemed to relax. They joked more often with each other and even made an effort to make Matt, Clarence, and Eveline more comfortable by throwing fresh hay in the back of the wagon. The food didn't improve—Hank was a lousy cook—and Matt was never really sure of what they were eating. Mostly stew, he figured, with contents he couldn't identify.

No matter how friendly things seemed, however, the ropes stayed securely bound on their wrists and ankles, and one of the slave hunters was always nearby to make sure they didn't escape. Matt couldn't forget the casual way Boss had backhanded him. He was black and, for that reason alone, was a slave. He was a piece of cargo that they were taking somewhere to sell like an animal. If they had to beat him to keep him in line, so be it. Fortunately, Matt was careful not to give them any reason to hit him again. But that didn't erase the painful memory—the burning shame—of being struck at all.

They cut across the black-bottomed land of western Tennessee, over gentle slopes, along swamps, and through endless woods of trees shorn of their red and yellow leaves. They glided past the fertile fields that, in their time, yielded lilies, orchids, wild rice, tobacco, corn, and the all-powerful cotton. They reached a town called Paris—"Named after Paris, France," Hank offered—where they got caught in a traffic jam of cows and pigs being brought in to market. Matt hoped this was the end of their trip. It wasn't. After giving the horses a rest and picking up supplies, they continued southeast to Danville, where they crossed the Tennessee River.

From the river, the land gave way to rolling bluegrass country and rich plateaus. Oaks and cedars rose high, their barely clothed limbs stretching up to the blue sky. Somewhere along the road, they stopped for the night, and Sonny announced that it was his intention one day to marry a girl from this part of Tennessee. "If I ever settle down, I'm settling right here," he said. "I'm gonna get me some

Tennessee land and raise some Tennessee horses and cure some Tennessee ham with Tennessee hickory and—"

"What in tarnation are you talking about?" Boss growled. "You're from Baltimore!"

Sonny shook his head mournfully and said, "I know it. But I should've been born in Tennessee."

The next day, they reached the Natchez Trace, where Hank felt duty-bound to inform his "ignorant passengers" about its importance. "It's one of the first roads ever made by the government. Goes all the way from Natchez, Mississippi, to Nashville, Tennessee. I saw a gunfight in Natchez once."

"Nobody cares," Boss said sleepily from under his hat.

Hank glanced around at their expressions and realized it was probably true. He settled back into a sulky silence.

One Sunday morning, nearly 12 days after they had left Odyssey, the hills of northern Alabama yielded to a valley where Huntsville sat waiting under the early sun. Matt noticed that Clarence began to get edgy, his eyes growing wide and dangerously wild as they got nearer to their destination. Eveline nestled closer to her father.

"What's wrong?" Matt whispered.

Clarence simply stared straight ahead and ignored the question.

"Eveline," Matt whispered again.

She slipped from her father's arms and leaned over to Matt. "No telling what Master Ramsay will do to us for running away," she whispered.

Matt felt like a fool for not realizing it sooner.

Hank laughed from the buckboard seat at the front of the wagon. "Well, now, I guess this is your Judgment Day—eh, Clarence?"

Boss, who had been on a horse ahead, whistled for Sonny to pick up their speed and follow him. Still north of town, they suddenly turned left onto a smaller road. A canopy of tree branches formed a natural tunnel that led to a large, white, two-storied mansion with pillars along the front, tall windows, and huge balconies. *It's straight out of "Gone with the Wind,"* Matt thought.

They drove around to the right of the house and followed a smaller path that took them into a compound of stables, workhouses, shacks, and, farther beyond toward the fields, a cluster of log houses.

"That's where we live," Eveline said with a catch in her throat.

Boss dismounted and walked up to the back door of the mansion. He shuffled from foot to foot as he rang the bell and waited. After a minute, the door opened, and a black servant appeared. Matt couldn't hear what Boss said to him, but the servant suddenly looked at the wagon, put his hand to his mouth with surprise, then disappeared into the house. Boss strolled back to the wagon.

"Well?" Sonny asked, crawling down from the buckboard seat and rubbing his rear. Hank did likewise.

"He's coming," Boss replied.

The door slammed, and Matt looked up in time to see a short man with a chiseled, white face and billowing housecoat race down the walkway.

"Boss! What're you doing here at this ungodly hour on a Sunday morning?" the man said. "Don't you know that—" He stopped himself when he saw Clarence and Eveline in the back of the wagon. "Good heavens, look at that!"

"I thought you'd be wanting your property back, Mr. Ramsay," Boss said.

Ramsay glared at Clarence and Eveline. "As a matter of interest, no, I don't want my property back. And it's taking every ounce of strength to keep from grabbing a horsewhip and driving these two troublemakers into the next county!"

Clarence refused to look Ramsay in the eyes. Eveline kept her gaze locked on her hands, which were neatly folded in her lap. Matt felt like throwing up.

"Wait now, Mr. Ramsay," Sonny gulped. "You say you don't want them back? But you put out a reward! You said you—"

"Oh, don't start sniveling," Ramsay said. "That doesn't mean you won't get money for them. Come into the kitchen, Boss. I have a proposition for you."

Boss followed Ramsay back up to the door, and the two of them went inside.

"This better not be some kind of trick," Hank snarled. He pointed a finger at Clarence. "If we don't get what's coming to us, I swear I'll skin you alive."

Fifteen minutes later, Boss returned to the wagon. Sonny and Hank watched him expectantly as he ran his fingers through his greasy hair, then put his hat on. "He doesn't want them," Boss reported. "He said they're too much trouble, trying to run away every chance they get. It's bad for the other slaves. Doesn't even want the boy."

Matt wasn't sure whether to feel relieved or insulted.

"So what's he want to do with them?" Hank asked.

"He's selling them to us."

"Us!" Sonny complained. "We don't have that kind of money."

"No—but we might in Huntsville. He wants us to sell them, and in return we'll give him part of what we make. I think it's a fair deal. We stand to make more from that than we would've just with the reward money."

"I'm not sure I like it," Hank said. "But I reckon we don't have much of a choice."

Sonny scratched his nose thoughtfully and said, "It suits me."

Boss came alongside the wagon and peered in at his three packages. "Did you get all that?" he asked.

Clarence and Eveline nodded. Matt looked perplexed. "I don't understand," he said. "What're you going to do with us?"

"I'm selling you, boy," Boss said earnestly. "Tomorrow you're gonna be on the auction block."

CHAPTER FIFTEEN

S unday was a slaves' day off for rest, going to church, or visiting nearby relatives. Since Clarence and Eveline were runaways, the overseer—a man named Watson who was in charge of the slaves—locked them up in an empty storeroom. Matt wasn't considered a threat, and Watson waved his hand at him in dismissal.

"But I have to talk to you," Matt said.

"You can go on," Watson snarled as he locked the door on Clarence and Eveline. "Go play or something."

"But I don't want to go play. I need to talk to somebody in charge. There's been a big mistake!"

Watson pushed him away. "You wanna talk to Mr. Ramsay? Forget it. Consider yourself fortunate that we're letting you stay here until the auction. It's not as if you belong to us."

"That's what I mean!" Matt persisted. "I don't belong to *anybody.* I don't belong here. I'm free."

"Leave me alone," Watson snapped and walked away.

Matt followed him. "Boss picked me up without having a right to. Don't you have laws against that? Somebody's going to be in big trouble. Understand? I'm *free!*"

"Shut up, boy," Watson said. "I don't want to know."

"But you *do* know."

They rounded the corner of a stable and nearly ran straight into Boss. He was brushing down his horse.

"What's wrong, Watson?" he asked casually.

"This boy says he's free, but you're selling him anyway," Watson replied.

"I am, and you know it!" Matt said.

"Shut up," Boss said to Matt.

Watson looked at Boss uneasily. "We don't want anything illegal going on here, Boss. Mr. Ramsay won't like it."

"There's nothing illegal about you putting up *my* slave for the night—as a favor."

"I'm not your slave!" Matt said.

Boss grabbed Matt by the shirt and yanked him so close to his face that Matt could smell yesterday's potatoes on his breath. He said softly, "You won't be *anybody's* slave if you don't close your mouth. That backhand I once gave you is nothing compared to what I'm willing to do." He thrust Matt away so hard that Matt fell and hit his head on a post.

"Do you have papers for him?" Watson asked.

Boss smiled and said, "I might have them around here somewhere. But you don't have to see them."

"Mr. Ramsay might ask."

"Only if someone gives him a reason to ask. I won't, and this boy won't—how about you?"

"Depends on what it's worth," Watson said.

Boss nodded, went to his saddlebag, and pulled out a pouch of coins. He fished around until he found an appropriate number and tossed them to Watson. "That should help to keep things quiet."

Watson considered the money and said, "I reckon it will."

Boss threw him another coin. "This is to help make sure the boy keeps quiet, too."

"Easily done," Watson said. He walked over to Matt, who was standing up. He put his hand on the leather handle of the whip attached to his belt. "Come on, boy," he ordered.

Matt looked at Boss's face, then Watson's, and realized what was going to happen. "No!" he said and tried to run in the opposite direction.

But Watson was too quick for him and had him by the collar instantly. Matt shouted. Watson gave him a hard thump on the back of the head with the end of his whip handle. Stunned, Matt began to cry. "No, no, no," he said over and over.

Watson dragged Matt back to the empty storehouse where Clarence and Eveline were held prisoners. He opened the door and shoved Matt inside. "Keep this boy quiet or the three of you won't live to regret it," he said to Clarence. He closed the door again and locked it.

Splinters of light came through the uneven boards on top of the shack. Matt lay on the ground and continued to cry. All his pent-up emotion had been unleashed and wouldn't be stopped. Eveline leaned down and held him close. "It's all right," she said gently.

Clarence also knelt down next to him and stroked his back. "Go ahead, Matthew," he said. "You go ahead and cry. Cry for all of us."

CHAPTER SIXTEEN

J ack sat in the steam train's passenger car at the Corinth railway station and stared at the Western Union Telegraph office across the platform. He fidgeted anxiously in the brown cloth seat. What was taking Reverend Andrew so long? he wondered.

It was yet another delay in what seemed like a trip of endless delays. First, they couldn't leave Odyssey until Reverend Andrew found someone to take his pulpit and pastoral responsibilities for a couple of weeks. That raised questions about *why* he was leaving, and though Andrew answered discreetly, word got back to the sheriff, who warned him not to try any of his "abolitionist stunts." Jack remembered well how the sheriff had squinted an eye and said, "I promise you, Reverend, that if you intentionally bring any runaways back to this town, there'll be more trouble than either one of us'll know how to handle."

The reverend politely thanked him for the warning.

Later that day, Jack and Andrew rode down to a wharf on the Mississippi and caught a riverboat headed south. Andrew insisted that he and Jack stay in their stateroom for the journey, since Jack's "obvious unfamiliarity with the ways of the riverboat" (he said) would make him stand out in a crowd. Jack suspected there were things on the riverboat that Andrew didn't approve of. The heavily made-up, perfumed women and the card games were probably two of those things, Jack guessed.

They made good time on the river until, just south of Cairo, Illinois, another boat had hit some river debris and blown up. Because of that, they were delayed a day getting to Columbus, Kentucky.

At Columbus, they took a train deeper into the South. Jack was surprised by the overall sootiness and dinginess of the steam train. The passenger cars were plain and box-like, with seats barely covered in thin fabric for marginal comfort. Jack had complained to Reverend Andrew about it. The reverend then informed him that some of the cars—particularly the ones the blacks were allowed to ride in—had hard, wooden seats. "Be grateful for what you have," he said.

Travel on the train was anything but smooth. There was a great deal of jolting and rocking, noise, and grating screeches. At night, the sparks from the engine flew past the dirty window like wild fireflies. Jack worried that the sparks might land on the wooden cars and turn to flames.

"You don't have to worry about that," Andrew said as he hooked a thumb toward the stove in the middle of the car.

"That'll start a fire long before the sparks will."

Jack wasn't comforted and didn't sleep much.

According to his plan, Andrew reminded Jack not to call him "Reverend" anymore. Now he was simply Andrew Ferguson or, to Jack, *Uncle* Andrew. He had given up his role as a minister and was now an ornithologist—a man who studied birds.

"Isn't that lying?" Jack had asked.

Andrew had smiled and said, "Not at all. Studying birds has been a hobby of mine for years. That I choose to omit the fact that I'm a northern minister who abhors slavery is no one's business but mine. We'll get onto the plantations to spread the word among the Alabama slaves about the Underground Railroad. Meanwhile, we'll look for your friend in Huntsville."

The plan seemed terribly simple to Jack. What if Matt wasn't in Huntsville? What if they took him somewhere else? What if they hurt him along the way?

They stopped at the station in Corinth, Mississippi, where they would then catch another train heading east to Huntsville. That's the train Jack was now sitting in. He squirmed in his seat and tugged at the collar of the shirt Andrew had bought for him. It was stiff and uncomfortable. The new, wool trousers also made his legs itch. And the shoes pinched his toes.

Andrew emerged from the telegraph office and leapt onto the train. He sat down across from Jack. "Well, that's done," he said.

"What did you do, Rev—er, *Uncle* Andrew?" Jack asked.

"I telegraphed ahead to a friend of mine in Huntsville. He'll help us when we arrive." He smiled and rubbed his hands together. "I'm quite pleased, Jack. If my estimations are correct, those slave hunters will only just be arriving with Clarence, Eveline, and your friend. I believe this excursion will yield much fruit for their freedom—and the freedom of others."

"Just so we find Matt," Jack said.

"Don't worry, lad. God is with us. What could go wrong?"

As soon as the words were out of his mouth, a man in a blue uniform and matching cap opened the door and poked his head into the train. "Sorry, gentlemen, but this train'll be delayed a few hours," he said.

"What!" Jack responded.

Andrew put a restraining hand on his knee. "What is the problem?" he asked the man.

The man scratched impatiently at his ear. "Train went off the track just outside of Decatur. Awful messy. Since it's the Sabbath, they can't rally the men they need to get it cleared until morning. Corinth's a nice little place. I'm sure you'll find lodgings."

"But what about Matt?" Jack asked.

CHAPTER SEVENTEEN

O n Monday morning, Boss took Matt, Clarence, and
Eveline to Huntsville. They had been given fresh
clothes to wear, for reasons Matt learned later. After
a half hour's drive, they made their way past the homes and
businesses on the outskirts of town to a cluster of rough,
wooden buildings. Several saddle horses were either tied or
held by servants as their owners assembled around a building
in the rear.

"This is the slave market," Clarence told Matt. While
Boss spoke to a bearded man over to the side, Sonny pulled
them off the back of the wagon and led them to a dozen
other slaves standing along a wide gate. As they walked,
Clarence took Matt's hand in one of his own. He held
Eveline's in the other. Matt's heart beat so fast that he
thought it might explode.

"Listen to me, son," Clarence whispered. "You've got to
learn to keep your mouth shut or you'll get sold to the worst

possible master. You hear? Because none of the nicer masters will want a black who is too big for his britches. Keep your eyes down—never look 'em full in the face—and just say yes, sir and no, sir."

"I'm afraid," Matt said.

"We all are," Clarence said.

Matt glanced around at the other slaves. They were men, women, and children of all sizes. Some clung to each other with tight fists and eyes wide and unblinking. They weren't dressed in the raggy work clothes that Matt expected but had on clothes given to them for the auction. The men had on black fur hats and coarse corduroy trousers, with nice vests and white cotton shirts. The women wore peasant dresses with scarves on their necks or over their heads. Clarence called them "market clothes"—which the slaves would be stripped of as soon as they were sold. That's why the three of them had been "dressed up": to make a good impression and bring a higher price.

On a signal, the slaves went through the gate into a narrow courtyard, where they were ranged in a semicircle for the white buyers to get a good look at them.

A woman fell to her knees and wept loudly, only to get a swift kick from the bearded man, who was obviously in charge of the day's business. He turned to the white buyers as if nothing had happened. "Good morning, gentlemen!" he said. "Would you like to examine this fine lot? It's as fine as ever came into a market!"

"This can't be happening," Matt said to himself.

The buyers moved down the line of blacks, looking them over from head to foot and checking their teeth and muscles as if they were horses or cattle. The slaves stood perfectly still.

A man with a goatee stepped up to Clarence, looked him over, then passed his gaze down to Eveline and Matt. "Is this a family?" he asked.

The bearded man nodded. "They are. For what service in particular did you want to buy?"

"I need a coachman," he replied.

"I have an excellent coachman right here," the bearded man said, stepping past Clarence to another slave. "He's strong and good-looking. A nice adornment to sit atop your coach."

The goateed man leaned forward to look at the slave. "What's your name?" he asked.

"George, sir."

"Step forward, George," the goateed man said. George obliged him. "How old are you?"

"I don't recollect," George replied. "I'm somewhere around 23."

"Where were you raised?"

"On Master Warner's farm in Virginny."

The man stroked his goatee. "Then you're a Virginia Negro."

"Yes, master, I'm a full-blooded Virginny."

"Did you drive your master's carriage?" he asked.

The slave nodded enthusiastically. "Yes, sir. I drove my

master's and my missus' carriage for more than four years."

"Have you got a wife?"

"I had one in Richmond and wish you would buy her, master, if you're going to buy me."

The goateed man grunted indifferently, then issued a series of orders like "Let me see your teeth and tongue. Open your hands. Roll up your sleeves. Have you got a good appetite? Are you good-tempered? Do you get sick very much?" He seemed satisfied by George's answers and finally said to the slave trader, "What are you asking for him?"

"He's worth a thousand dollars, but I'll take 975."

The goateed man talked him down to $950.

Just as the deal was concluded, another man named Mason stepped forward and thumped Clarence in the chest. "He's a sound one," Mason said. "I'll take him."

The slave trader smiled and said, "Oh, he's a good one, all right. A hard worker and—"

Mason turned on the slave trader with a cold look. "Don't butter me up," he said. "I know this slave belonged to Mr. Ramsay and is notorious for running away. But I'll get that notion out of his head. I'll give you $850."

The bearded slave trader looked over at Boss, who'd been standing quietly by the courtyard fence. Boss nodded. "Sold!" the slave trader announced happily.

"Come along, boy," Mason said.

Clarence hesitated.

The slave trader grabbed Clarence by the collar and pushed him along. "You heard him. Go," he ordered.

But Clarence couldn't go far, because Eveline and Matt held firmly to his hands.

"What's this?" Mason asked angrily.

The slave trader punched out at Eveline and Matt to make them let go. He caught Matt in the side and knocked the wind out of him. Matt slumped to the ground.

"No, no!" Eveline cried.

"Don't lose your head," Clarence told her. "You know how to behave."

Eveline stubbornly held on to her father's hand. "Please!" she cried.

The slave trader struck out at her with both fists, sending her to the ground. Clarence spun around with wild eyes. A whip cracked the morning sky like a gunshot, and all Matt could see was the expression of agonizing pain on Clarence's face.

"You're coming with me, boy," Mason shouted as he prepared his whip for another strike. Clarence leaned down to his daughter and said only "Behave" before he stumbled after Mason.

"Lord Jesus, help me!" Eveline cried. Matt, still winded, crawled over to her and put his arms around her.

The slave trader stepped forward, his teeth grinding with anger. "You young ones need a lesson, I think," he said. He started to kick at them with his pointy-toed boot. Matt threw himself between the trader and Eveline to take most of the blows.

"Stop it! Stop it right now!" someone shouted.

The kicking suddenly stopped as the slave trader backed away. "Yes, Colonel," he said obediently.

Colonel Alexander Ross knelt down next to Matt and Eveline. "Can you sit up?" he asked gently.

Matt nodded and, with aching ribs, sat up. Eveline wiped away her tears and did the same.

"What a brave boy you must be," Colonel Ross said to Matt. Then he gestured to the slave trader and said, "I want them."

Matt looked away to keep him from seeing the tears gathering in his eyes.

"For what service, Colonel?" the slave trader asked.

"House servants," he answered. "What's their price?"

"Normally I would ask—"

"I'll *give* you $500 for the two of them."

Once again the slave trader looked at Boss. Boss slowly nodded. "Five hundred it is, Colonel," the slave trader said.

The colonel helped them both to their feet. "Come on, children. You're coming home with me," he said with a smile.

CHAPTER EIGHTEEN

J ack and Andrew arrived in Huntsville close to noon. At the Liberty Hotel, a telegram was waiting for Andrew. He opened the envelope, read the message, and then leaned against the counter with a grimace.

"What's wrong?" Jack asked.

"My friend investigated Mr. Ramsay's stock of slaves and learned through the overseer that Clarence, Eveline, and Matthew were taken to the slave market," he said. He folded the telegram and shoved it into his coat pocket. "That's a setback. I wouldn't have expected Ramsay to dispose of them so quickly."

"What do we do? We have to find them!" Jack said, his worst fear becoming a reality.

Andrew nodded and turned to inquire casually if the clerk knew of any slave markets taking place that day.

"I'm not entirely certain," the clerk replied. He then held up his hand and turned to a black porter nearby. "How about it, Sam? Do you know of any markets going on today?"

Sam replied, "Well, sir, Monday is usually a good day for buying. But I heard of only one market, and that was this morning."

"Are you sure?" Andrew asked.

"Yes, sir," Sam answered. "My cousin Ishom was to be sold there."

"Take us," Andrew said.

Sam looked to the clerk for permission. The clerk shrugged and said, "At the usual rate."

On the street, Sam flagged them a carriage, climbing up next to the driver while Jack and Andrew got into the back. They made their way through the city streets at a speed that Jack thought might drive him crazy. He kept looking out the window just in case he could spot Matt in the business-day crowds. At one junction he did see something that caught his eye.

"Look!" he shouted to Andrew.

Andrew leaned over. "What?" he asked.

"That wagon. Aren't those the slave hunters from Odyssey?"

As Andrew got into a better position to look, the wagon turned out of sight. "Missed it," he said.

Jack wiped the sweat from his brow. "It was them. I swear it was them."

"Then perhaps we're closer than we could've hoped."

The carriage weaved through the traffic to a less-crowded area of town. The driver pulled up to a cluster of brown buildings that Jack would've called shacks.

"This is the place," Sam said, leaning down from the driver's seat. "That courtyard yonder."

Jack and Andrew climbed down from the carriage. Jack nearly ran to the wide gate, but Andrew put a firm hand on his shoulder. "Not so fast," he whispered. "You can't look too interested."

They walked to the gate, opened it on creaky hinges, and stepped into the empty yard. On the opposite end, a bearded man spied them and waved. "Hello!" he called and crossed over to them.

"Greetings," Andrew said. "Is this the slave market?"

"One of them," the man said. "The only one today."

Andrew smiled and said, "I see. What time may we have the pleasure of seeing your . . . your slaves?"

"Nine o'clock this morning," the man replied.

"We missed it?" Jack asked anxiously.

The man looked at Jack as if surprised that he would speak. "Yes, you did," he said.

"Did you have a man with a boy and girl about my age?" Jack asked quickly.

The question raised the man's eyebrows. "We have a lot of men, boys, and girls. Women, too. What's your interest?" The man's tone was suspicious.

Andrew cleared his throat and said, "We had heard of three particularly valuable slaves from Mr. Ramsay's plantation. We're sorry we missed the opportunity to buy them, that's all."

The man eyed them carefully. "Well, they were here—and they've been sold."

"Sold!" Jack shouted.

"Oh, dear. And we've come all this way," Andrew said with mock unhappiness. "May we ask to whom they were sold?"

"I don't remember," the man said, but he gestured so subtly that Jack almost missed it. He rubbed his fingers together.

Andrew sniffed casually, reached into his waistcoat pocket, and retrieved a couple of coins. Then he handed them to the bearded man.

****

Back at the hotel, Jack and Andrew entered their room. No sooner was the door closed than Andrew grabbed Jack by the arm.

"Hey!" Jack cried out, startled.

"Listen to me, young man," Andrew said sharply. "Our lives—and the lives of many others—depend on our being as unassuming as possible. We cannot draw attention to ourselves. No one must ever suspect that we're up to anything unusual or everything we hope to accomplish will be completely destroyed. For that reason, you must *keep your mouth shut in public and do only what I tell you to do.* Do you understand?"

"Yes, Uncle Andrew," Jack said.

"Good," Andrew said and let him go. "We'll have to pray the slave trader doesn't run back to his customers and tell them about our questions."

"But you paid him!"

Andrew unbuttoned his shirt and toyed with a necklace just beneath. "I paid him for some *answers.* I'm not so optimistic that it will also keep him from talking."

Jack dropped himself into a particularly uncomfortable chair. "This is a disaster," he said. "They've been sold. And not just sold—they've been sold to two separate people! How are we supposed to rescue them now?"

Andrew tugged at the necklace, and Jack saw that it held a small, silver cross. "By faith, Jack," he said. "We'll rescue them by faith."

Andrew turned away from Jack and poured water from a pitcher into a bowl. He began to wash his face and neck. Jack dropped his chin onto his fist and, as he did, suddenly felt a strange, tickling sensation go through his stomach. *Butterflies,* he thought. *I'm feeling nervous about Matt.*

But the butterflies flew on, and Jack felt a weird surge through his body as if he were on a roller-coaster ride. He tried to stand up but couldn't. Alarmed, he called out to Reverend Andrew, who suddenly spun away from him— along with the room and the light—into darkness.

"What's going on here?" a deep, warm voice echoed in the darkness.

****

At that same moment, Matt was on the back of a wagon, trying to comfort Eveline. She hadn't stopped crying since they had left the slave auction and drove away toward the colonel's plantation.

"They took my daddy, they took my daddy," she wept again and again.

His sides still hurting, Matt winced as he leaned close to her. "Don't worry," he said. "We'll find him."

"How?" Eveline sniffed.

"I don't know," Matt said. "But we will. I promise."

She put her head against his arm. "Promise?"

"Yeah," Matt replied as he leaned his head against the coarse siding of the wagon. He closed his eyes wearily. His stomach lurched as if the wagon had suddenly slipped into a dip in the road. And that's when he heard the voice.

"What's going on here?" it asked.

It was so close that Matt thought someone had whispered in his ear. He opened his eyes while his stomach continued to do flips. Of course, he expected to see Eveline and the back of the wagon they'd been riding on. Instead, he found himself looking at a flashing red light.

CHAPTER NINETEEN

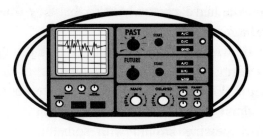

W ell?" the voice asked again.

"Who's there? Where are you?" Jack asked, still not able to see anyone. He was aware that his right arm felt prickly, as if it had fallen asleep. He pushed out with it and hit someone.

"Ouch! Cut it out!"

Jack turned a little, and in the glow of a flashing red light, he saw the outline of a face. "Matt?"

"Yeah, it's me," Matt answered. "I'm waiting for my stomach to settle down."

"Me, too. And I'm *really* confused," Jack said.

"So am I. How did we get here?"

"I don't know. I'm not sure where *here* is. Did you hear that voice?" Jack asked.

"Uh huh. Are we home?" Matt *didn't* sound happy.

The voice bounced around them again. "Jack? Matt? Are you in there?"

"It's Mr. Whittaker!" Jack said, elated. "We're here!"

With a *whoosh,* the door to The Imagination Station slid open. Light assaulted Jack and Matt so that they winced and had to lean back and cover their eyes.

Whit stood with his hands on his hips and a disapproving look on his normally friendly face. "Come out of there," he said. "I want to know what the two of you are doing in my machine without permission. Don't you realize how dangerous it is—messing around with something you don't understand? What if it locked you in and I didn't come back down as soon as I did?"

Jack sheepishly crawled out, explaining as he did, "We didn't know what it was. See, we were playing behind Whit's End and found the tunnel, and it led to here and we saw the machine, and . . ." Jack's voice trailed off as he realized Whit was looking beyond him.

"Matt?" Whit called out.

Jack turned around to see that Matt was still inside The Imagination Station. "Come on, Matt," Jack insisted.

"No," Matt said in a small voice. "I can't."

Whit cocked one of his bushy, white eyebrows and said, "You can't?"

"No, sir."

"Why not?"

"Because I promised," Matt said with a sniffle from the shadow of the machine.

Jack was surprised to realize that Matt had a choked, crying sound in his voice.

"*What* did you promise?" Whit asked.

"I promised Eveline that I would help her find her father."

"Eveline?"

"The slave girl," Jack explained. "She and Clarence were captured by the slave hunters and taken to Alabama. They took Matt, too. Reverend Andrew and I followed them."

Matt continued from inside the machine, "They sold Clarence to another plantation, then sold me and Eveline to some colonel. She was crying, Mr. Whittaker, and I promised. Please don't make me leave them there."

Whit stroked his mustache for a moment, then strolled over to his workbench. "That's not how the story went," he said as he picked up one of the books lying there.

"Story?" Jack asked.

"I've been programming The Imagination Station to play out different kinds of stories—from the Bible and from history." He flipped a few pages in the book, then turned to Jack. "I had set The Imagination Station in its program mode to input all kinds of information, including Clarence's and Eveline's story. They had been caught by the slave hunters here at Whit's End and taken south—"

"Just like we said!"

"Yes, but they weren't sold to separate slave owners in the original story. They were both sold to Colonel Alexander Ross. Later, Reverend Andrew showed up posing as an ornithologist—"

"Yeah! I was with Reverend Andrew!" Jack said

excitedly. "I was his assistant!"

Whit shook his head. "It's very strange. You must have come in right after I went upstairs. I've only been gone for 15 minutes."

"Fifteen minutes!" Jack cried out. "We've been in there for almost two weeks!"

Whit scrubbed his chin and explained, "The adventures work at an accelerated pace."

Jack couldn't believe it. "Wow," was all he could figure to say.

Whit continued, "But what doesn't make sense to me is why the story has changed." He fell silent for a moment, then suddenly snapped his fingers. "You two must have gotten into The Imagination Station while it was in the *middle* of inputting the program! Your interference changed the story."

Jack felt as though Whit was blaming them for something, but he didn't understand enough of what Whit had just said to know for sure.

"You mean we messed it up?" Matt asked.

Whit leaned against the door to The Imagination Station and peered in at Matt. "It looks that way."

That's what happens when you do things you're not supposed to do.

Though Whit didn't say those actual words, Jack and Matt both felt the sting as if he had.

Matt got that choked sound in his voice again as he said, "But what's it mean? Are Clarence and Eveline in trouble because of us?"

Whit shrugged and said, "By getting into the machine when you did, you changed the program—and that must have changed the story."

"Then we have to go back and fix it," Matt said urgently.

"It's only a story, Matt," Whit said.

"No, it isn't! It was real! *They* were real. You have to let me go back. I promised I'd help!" Matt's voice was high-pitched and panicked.

Whit gazed at Matt warmly, his eyes soft with understanding. "You're taking this pretty seriously," he said gently.

"I promised," Matt said quietly.

Whit turned to Jack. "You, too?"

Jack nibbled on his lower lip, then nodded. "Yeah. Reverend Andrew was counting on me to help," he said with more confidence than he felt.

"Reverend Andrew's mission—and what happened to Clarence and Eveline—took a lot of courage. It won't be easy," Whit told them.

"It wasn't easy before," Matt said.

Whit glanced at his watch as if to confirm that they still had time enough to do it. He then waved his hand for Jack to get back into the machine. "Go on," he said. "But I'll be watching you closely this time. And when you're finished, we're going to have a talk about you sneaking in here in the first place."

Jack settled into the seat next to Matt again. Matt turned his face away, embarrassed that he had become so emotional.

"Just push the red button when you're ready," Whit said

as the door closed.

"We have to be out of our minds to go back," Jack said in the darkness.

"Yeah, we probably are," Matt agreed.

Then Matt reached forward and pushed down on the flashing red button.

To Be Continued

About the Author

Paul McCusker is producer, writer, and director for the Adventures in Odyssey audio series. He is also the author of a variety of popular plays including *The First Church of Pete's Garage, Pap's Place,* and co-author of *Sixty-Second Skits* (with Chuck Bolte).

Don't Miss a Single
"Adventures in Odyssey" Novel!

Strange Journey Back
Mark Prescott hates being a newcomer in the small town of Odyssey. And he's not too thrilled about his only new friend being a girl. That is, until Patti tells him about a time machine at Whit's End called The Imagination Station. With hopes of using the machine to bring his separated parents together again, Mark learns a valuable lesson about friendship and responsibility.

High Flyer with a Flat Tire
Joe Devlin is accusing Mark of slashing the tire on his new bike. Mark didn't do it, but how can he prove his innocence? Only by finding the real culprit! With the help of his wise friend, Whit, Mark untangles the mystery and learns new lessons about friendship and family ties.

The Secret Cave of Robinwood
Mark promises his friend Patti that he will never reveal the secret of her hidden cave. But when a gang Mark wants to join is looking for a new clubhouse, Mark thinks of the cave. Will he risk his friendship with Patti? Through the adventure, Mark learns about the need to belong and the gift of forgiveness.

Behind the Locked Door
Why does Mark's friend Whit keep his attic door locked? What's hidden up there? While staying with Whit, Mark grows curious when he's forbidden to go behind the locked door. It's a hard-learned lesson about trust and honesty.

Lights Out at Camp What-a-Nut
At camp, Mark finds out he's in the same cabin with Joe Devlin, Odyssey's biggest bully. And when Mark and Joe are paired in a treasure hunt, they plunge into unexpected danger and discover how God uses one person to help another.

The King's Quest
Mark is surprised and upset to find he must move back to Washington, D.C. He feels like running away. And that's exactly what The Imagination Station enables him to do! With Whit's help, he goes on a quest for the king

to retrieve a precious ring. Through the journey, Mark faces his fears and learns the importance of obeying authority and striving for eternal things.

Danger Lies Ahead
Jack Davis knew he was off to a bad start when he saw a moving van in front of Mark's house, heard that an escaped convict could be headed toward Odyssey, and found himself sent to the principal's office—all on the first day of school! Thrown headfirst into the course of chaos, Jack's imagination runs overtime. Will it cost him his friendships with Oscar and Lucy?

Point of No Return
Turning over a new leaf isn't as easy as Jimmy Barclay thought it would be. And when his friends abandon him, his grandmother falls ill, and the only kid who seems to understand what he's going through moves away, he begins to wonder, "Does God really care?" Through the challenges, Jimmy discovers that standing up for what you believe in can be costly—and rewarding!

Other Works by the Author

NOVELS:
Strange Journey Back (Focus on the Family)
High Flyer with a Flat Tire (Focus on the Family)
Secret Cave of RobinWood (Focus on the Family)
Behind the Locked Door (Focus on the Family)
Lights Out at Camp What-a-Nut (Focus on the Family)
The King's Quest (Focus on the Family)
Danger Lies Ahead (Focus on the Family)
Point of No Return (Focus on the Family]
Time Twists: Sudden Switch (Chariot/Lion)
Time Twists: Stranger in the Mist (Chariot/Lion)
Time Twists: Memory's Gate (Chariot/Lion)
You Say Tomato (with Adrian Plass; HarperCollins UK)

INSTRUCTIONAL:
Youth Ministry Comedy & Drama:
      Better Than Bathrobes But Not Quite Broadway
      (with Chuck Bolte; Group Books)
Playwriting:
      A Study in Choices & Challenges (Lillenas)

SKETCH COLLECTIONS:
Batteries Not Included (Baker's Plays)
Fast Foods (Monarch UK)
Drama for Worship, Vol. 1: On the Street Interview (Word)
Drama for Worship, Vol. 2: The Prodigal & the Pig Farmer (Word)
Drama for Worship, Vol. 3: Complacency (Word)
Drama for Worship, Vol. 4: Conversion (Word)
Quick Skits and Discussion Starters (with Chuck Bolte; Group Books)
Sixty-Second Skits (with Chuck Bolte; Group Books)
Short Skits for Youth Ministry (with Chuck Bolte; Group Books)
Sketches of Harvest (Baker's Plays)
Souvenirs (Baker's Plays)
Vantage Points (Lillenas)
Void Where Prohibited (Baker's Plays)

PLAYS:
The Case of the Frozen Saints (Baker's Plays)
The First Church of Pete's Garage (Baker's Plays)
The Revised Standard Version of Jack Hill (Baker's Plays)
A Work in Progress (Lillenas)
Camp W (CDS)
Catacombs (Lillenas)
Death by Chocolate (Baker's Plays)
Family Outings (Lillenas)
Father's Anonymous (Lillenas)
Pap's Place (Lillenas)
Snapshots & Portraits (Lillenas)

MUSICALS:
The Meaning of Life & Other Vanities (with Tim Albritton; Baker's Plays)
Shine the Light of Christmas (with Dave and Jan Williamson; Word Music)
A Time for Christmas
      (with David Clydesdale, Steve Amerson, Lowell Alexander; Word Music)